The Heart Match

MAPLE GARDENS MATCHMAKERS
BOOK ONE

PHILLIPA NEFRI CLARK

The Heart Match

Cover by Wynter Designs

The Heart Match

Chapter One

Isobel Davis darted down the busy Atlanta street and darted inside her favorite coffee shop. *Just Peachy* was a newer establishment and was a hidden gem in the downtown area. It was also the only place that gave out free newspapers during the week.

Tossing a smile at Ava behind the counter, Izzie headed across the room toward the stack of newspapers and swiped the one on top. She flicked it open, her eyes sweeping through the classifieds.

Yes! There was an estate sale that weekend. There hadn't been one of those in a while. Maybe her mother's jade necklace would be there. The universe had dumped so much hardship on her family, she was due for a miracle.

Izzie folded the newspaper and tucked it under her arm. She wove through the tables and chairs.

"Where do you think you're going?"

Standing frozen in place, Izzie pressed her lips into a thin line and closed her eyes. Maybe Ava was talking to someone else? She really was too much of a chatter box and Izzie had a long list of things to do before work. She tossed a glance over her shoulder to find Ava's amused blue eyes drilling into her.

"You can't just come in here, take a newspaper, and sneak out like a stray cat."

Izzie giggled. "Stray cat? You *know* I would stay to chat if I could, but I had to take an extra shift this morning and I have to visit my mom."

Ava flipped her blonde hair over her shoulder then leaned on the counter. Her lower lip puckered into a pout. "We haven't had a good girl's talk in ages. You work too hard. When are you going to realize that you should only work to live, not live to work?"

Izzie cocked her head to the side. "I think you got that wrong. Isn't it eat to live rather than live to eat?"

Ava shrugged. "I like mine better." She straightened and a smirk touched her perfect lips. "Regardless, we should plan a girl's night."

"I'll let you know when I have time," Izzie waved at her. "Thanks for the newspaper."

"That defeats the purpose—"

The door cut off her friend's words and Izzie hurried down the road to her car. She had an hour and a half before she needed to be at work. That gave her just enough time to eat breakfast with her mother.

She made it to the beat-up yellow Volkswagen Bug that was parked a few yards away and yanked on the handle. The door stuck, as it usually did, forcing her to pull three more times before it released. Izzie stumbled back a step to catch her balance then jumped into her car and turned the key.

The drive out to Maple Gardens Assisted Living wasn't bad. It was about a twenty-minute drive from Atlanta to get to the fancy retirement community, and only because it was out in the middle of nowhere. The whole place was surrounded by maple trees as far as the eye could see. Driving down the winding road toward the hub of the community always made her feel like she was entering a fairytale land.

Flecks of light burst through the leaves overhead, dancing on her windows as she passed beneath the trees on either side of her road. At the end of the road, a large brick building rose from the earth. The main structure was for the residents who needed more care than the average tenants. It was where her mother currently resided. Surrounding that building were several other smaller apartment blocks.

Izzie drove past trails where elderly couples wandered with their spouses, health care workers, or their adult children. There was a degree of peace, just passing the threshold onto the property. It was the reason she'd picked this community for her mother despite the high price point, and the reason she'd added more hours to her weekly work schedule.

She pulled into the visitor's parking lot, snatched her newspaper, jumped out of her car, and sprinted toward the main building. The automatic doors glided open, revealing the front reception desk.

Olivia's familiar raven-haired head popped up and she smiled widely. "Izzie! Your mom's been asking for you. We weren't sure you were going to make it today." She stood behind the desk and murmured something at the other receptionist before coming out and meeting Izzie. Her grey eyes dropped to the newspaper under Izzie's arm. "Any luck today?"

Izzie's head bobbed as she walked with her best friend down the familiar hallway toward her mother's room. "I have a good feeling about this one, Livy. It's a local estate sale and the notice said there was a lot of jewelry."

Olivia's eyes brightened. "That's wonderful! Are you going to tell your mother about it?"

The happiness in Izzie's countenance dimmed. "No. I don't think that would be a very good idea." They shifted to the side of the hallway, making room for a woman pushing a resident in a wheelchair. "She's been disappointed too many times."

Her friend nodded, lips pressed in a thin line. "That's probably a good plan." They stopped outside of a familiar door. The name on the small plaque on the wall read *Davis*.

Izzie gestured toward the room. "How's she doing this morning?"

Olivia's eyes darted to the door then back to Izzie's face. She tilted her head slightly and offered a soft smile. "Okay, I think. She kept asking about you. But she was in good spirits."

"Have you heard if she's making any more progress?"

This time Olivia's features faltered. She reached out and touched Izzie's upper arm. "I think she's made as much progress as they expected. More, even. At this point we just have to be happy with how far she's come."

Izzie swallowed hard and nodded. "You're right. I know you're right. I just wish..." She glanced at the closed door.

"I know, sweetie." Olivia wrapped her arms around Izzie then pulled back and grinned. "Let me know how that estate sale goes."

Izzie nodded again and headed into her mother's room.

Margaret was already seated in her wheelchair staring out the window at the gardens within her view. She twisted, glancing over her shoulder and a wide smile stretched from ear to ear. "Izzie! You're here."

Warmth spread through Izzie's body as she wandered across the room. "Of course I'm here. I told you I'd eat breakfast with you every morning." Her hands settled on the wheelchair. "Not to mention, we have to finish that chapter in Pride and Prejudice."

If it was possible, her mother's features brightened further. "Ooh, I love that one."

She placed the book in her mother's lap. "I know, mom." Izzie grinned as she turned her mother's chair around and rolled her out the door. "Do you remember where we are in the story?"

Her mother grew still except for her fingers which fidgeted with the book in her lap. She murmured something Izzie couldn't understand.

"It's okay, mom. I'll help you remember." They headed down the hall toward the cafeteria. Some of the workers wearing scrubs waved animatedly at Margaret, wishing her a good morning. But most of the residents they passed weren't completely lucid, so when her mother waved at them, they didn't respond.

Izzie frowned. Her mother's memory was the *only* reason she hadn't been moved into one of the other buildings. There were other tenants who had mobility issues and they weren't required to have such strict supervision. If only she could get her mother to crest that threshold.

They arrived in the cafeteria and Izzie paused. "Where do you want to sit this morning?"

Her mother surveyed the room, from one side to the other. "I don't see Lawrence."

"Lawrence?" Izzie stared down at the top of her mother's head. Last time they'd shared a meal, Margaret couldn't remember Lawrence. The two had met one another two weeks ago and the nurses kept putting them together—

something to do with how bright and happy her mother was. She seemed to share some of her light with the other resident. "You remember Lawrence?"

Margaret glanced up at her, a grin on her face. "Of course I remember Lawrence, dear. He's my dear friend."

Izzie couldn't dare hope that this was the turning point she'd been praying for. Her mother hadn't been able to make new memories very well. Even some of the older ones were hard to dig up. Heart beating a little faster, Izzie spun her mother around. "Well, I guess we should go find your friend, then, shouldn't we?"

They headed for the reception desk, but Olivia wasn't there. The other woman offered them a smile. "What can I do for you?"

Izzie ran a hand through her auburn hair and shifted her weight from one foot to the other. "My mom wants to eat breakfast with one of the other residents. Do you think you could find him?" This could very well be against the rules.

"Of course. Anything for Margaret." The woman winked at Izzie's mother.

Izzie blinked. "Oh. Great."

"Who are we looking for?"

"Lawrence." Her mother offered.

The receptionist turned to her computer and clicked a few times. "It looks like his nephew checked him out this morning but he said they'd be staying on the grounds. You might be able to find them out in the commons."

"Hear that mom? Lawrence might be in the commons. What do you say about breakfast outside?"

"That sounds lovely dear."

Izzie looked up at the receptionist. "Thank you." They turned and headed out the door into the warm morning sunlight. They took a left and made their way toward the large open area surrounded by shrubs and greenery. A few wrought iron tables were situated in the center near a bubbling fountain and several benches lined the perimeter.

Her mother sat straighter in her chair and pointed. "There he is. There's Lawrence."

Izzie's eyes followed her mother's gesture and she peered across the way. Then her blood ran cold. "Oh, Mom. I don't think today is a good day. He looks busy, visiting with someone." She made to turn the wheelchair around but her mother threw her hands onto the brakes, making it harder to go anywhere. "*Mom*. We can visit with him another—"

"*No*. I want to eat breakfast with Lawrence." Her mother set a pair of earnest eyes on Izzie. "He's my friend, Izzie. Please."

Izzie's shoulders slumped as she stared at her mother then over to where Lawrence sat on a bench beside someone she would have recognized anywhere. Lawrence's nephew was none other than Bartholomew Brown—heir apparent to the fortune of his uncle. Playboy. Adventurer. And drop dead gorgeous.

One more attempt at turning around got her nowhere. Her mother wasn't going to budge. Izzie expelled a sigh from her lips. "Fine. Let's go say hi to Lawrence." They bumped along the cobblestone path toward the elderly man. Izzie kept her gaze averted, not prepared to meet the eyes that had stared at her from magazines at the convenience store where she worked.

They arrived far too soon. Margaret beamed at Lawrence and his nephew. Lawrence didn't acknowledge their presence while his nephew gazed at them with curiosity.

Izzie leaned over and murmured, "Let's come back another time."

"No, Izzie. Lawrence, you don't mind us sitting with you, do you?" Margaret beamed at Lawrence and waved at his visitor, her paperback copy of *Pride and Prejudice* flying out of her hands.

Bartholomew Brown got to it just before Izzie, scooping it off the grass in one fluid motion and holding it out with a smile. He was taller than she expected. And it was obvious he spent time at the gym, those broad muscular shoulders easily visible beneath his fitted t-shirt. *Stop it!* Izzie dragged her eyes to his face.

That was a very bad idea. Warm brown eyes regarded her with amusement.

She cleared her throat. "Um, thanks."

"Shall I return it to your mother?"

"It's Margaret." Her mother chimed in. "Izzie, get the book, dear."

Right, he was still holding it out to her. She curled her fingers around the edge farthest from his fingers. "I'll take it."

"I'm Bart."

"I know."

"The normal response is, 'And I'm Izzie'."

She froze. "How do you know my name?"

8

Chapter Two

Bart bit back a chuckle that wanted to fly from his mouth. He arched a brow. "Your mother just said it."

A blush filled her cheeks. "It's Isobel, actually." She tugged on the book he still held. "May I have this please?"

He released the book and nodded toward Margaret, who'd positioned her wheelchair beside the bench. She was deeply invested in a one-sided conversation. "She cheers him up."

Izzie's eyes darted toward her mother. "She loves talking to him, even if he can't answer. But I think he does, in his own way."

Lawrence blinked faster as Margaret laughed at her own joke. Bart's smile widened. "I think you're right." He folded his strong arms across his chest and shifted his weight from one foot to the other. His voice lowered to a murmur. "The stroke left him a shell of his former self. You read to him, don't you?"

Izzie glanced at him and tucked a strand of red hair behind her ear. "Mom forgets a lot since her accident, so I read her some of the books she used to love reading." Her smile was soft and warm, drawing his attention as she continued. "I think he likes them, too."

Bart leaned a little closer toward her, causing her to stumble back a step. His smile remained as he murmured. "Thank you."

"For reading to them? It's a little thing." She touched her hair again, her eyes darting away then meeting his again before Izzie hurried to Margaret. She dropped onto the bench between her mother's wheelchair and Lawrence. "All right. I only have thirty minutes. Let's see if Darcy finally admits he's in love with Elizabeth."

Bart watched with rapt curiosity as the beautiful red-head dove into the story she held at her lap. The nurse had mentioned Lawrence had a new friend. He hadn't expected to come across her so soon, nor that she'd have a beautiful daughter.

He rubbed his jaw then turned around in search of a chair. There was a vacant one that sat beside a table not too far from where his uncle seemed to have perked up. It was amazing, the affect she had on him. Bart settled into the chair and leaned over, resting his elbows on his knees. His hands dangled over the edge of his legs as he listened to her voice.

She had a natural kind of prettiness about her that he didn't see all that often over at the casino. Her auburn hair glinted in the sunlight and her eyes seemed to flash with a shrewd sense of intelligence. Most of the women who ended up coming through the doors to his world seemed to wear too much makeup and wear clothes that revealed a little too much. Granted, a good majority of those he spent time with were performers in the theater his uncle had put in shortly before his stroke.

Izzie wasn't like them at all. If he had to compare her

mannerisms to someone, the closest person he could come up with would be that princess who got locked away with that beast.

And just like that, the thirty minutes were up. Izzie hopped up from her place on the bench, grabbed her mother's wheelchair, and reminded her to say her goodbyes.

Bart got to his feet, stepping into her path. She stopped abruptly, causing her mother to lurch slightly. Margaret twisted in her seat and gave her daughter a look. "Careful, Izzie. You nearly ran over this nice young man." She turned around and looked up at him. "She can be in such a hurry sometimes."

Why did he just block her? What was he going to say? *Don't go*? That would have sounded weird. He offered Margaret a smile and stepped out of the way. "It was completely my fault. Sorry." He met Izzie's guarded expression. "I'll see you around sometime, Izzie."

"It's Isobel," Izzie murmured as she walked past.

He turned, watching her walk away. Did he do something wrong? Usually the women he interacted with were more... more what exactly? Flirty? Warm? But not Izzie. She was more consumed with something else. Maybe it had something to do with her mother. Serious. That's what it was. Someone as young as she appeared to be didn't need to be so serious. It made him want to know exactly what was going on in her life to make her so somber.

His brows furrowed as he turned toward his uncle. Lawrence had that blank stare on his face again. The little bit of coherency he'd shown when he was with Margaret was now gone. There was something about the Davis women that had woken him up to a small degree—one more reason he wanted to get to know them more.

Bart wandered over to his uncle and groaned as he

settled onto the bench beside him. "How are you feeling today, Uncle Lawrence?"

Of course he wouldn't answer. He hadn't spoken a word since he'd had his stroke. The most they ever got were facial expressions. Bart leaned back and draped his arm on the bench behind his uncle. "I have a buyer for all but one of your casinos. Everything should close by the end of next month if it goes according to plan. I'm keeping your first one, though. And all profits will go to the charities you supported."

He glanced at his uncle out of the corner of his eye. Nothing. No acknowledgement of their conversation. Bart sighed. He didn't even know why he talked. It seemed strange. Uncle Lawrence hadn't even really spent much time with him when he was younger. Being given all of his uncle's holdings had been a shock not only to his mother but to the rest of the family.

"So what do you think of those Davis women?"

His uncle didn't react.

"Margaret seems nice. She talks a lot though."

Bart could have sworn his uncle's mouth twitched. But he must have been mistaken. Lawrence didn't move. Just like always. "I bet you like listening to Izzie as much as I do. I hope she comes back and reads to you often. That was really nice of her."

His gaze swept through the property, bouncing from resident to resident before he shifted his focus once again to his uncle. "I have a meeting with Isaac later today. I think he wants me to remain on the board for this place." He rubbed the back of his neck. "But I don't know if I want any of this." Bart heaved a sigh and shifted, leaning over and resting his elbows on his knees. "This isn't the life I had expected to lead. But I feel like if I don't stick around, your legacy will be lost."

Bart glanced at his uncle out of the corner of his eye once more. What was he thinking? This conversation wasn't going to do a lick of good. He could be reading to his uncle from the stocks in the newspaper and he'd get the same effect.

No one else in his family bothered to visit Lawrence. It was like they'd all washed their hands of the man when they found out he hadn't given any of his wealth to them.

He stared at his uncle. "Why?"

Lawrence blinked.

"Why did you pick me? I don't get it. I have no idea what I'm doing. You should have asked someone else. Anyone else. Heck, Isaac would have been better at handling all of this." He blew out a breath and shook his head. "I just wish I knew."

Bart got to his feet and brushed off his suit pants. "I'll see you again later this week, Uncle Lawrence. Have a good day."

Bart sat in the familiar conference room where he'd spent a lot of his time over the last several months. No one had come in to speak with him and he'd been there for at least twenty minutes. Granted, this wasn't a big board meeting. It was just supposed to be a meeting between Isaac and himself, but for what, he didn't know.

He pushed out his chair and walked over to the window. He wasn't equipped to be the CEO of his uncle's estate, so he'd kept Isaac on. Hopefully this didn't have something to do with stepping down. Bart didn't know if he could manage any of this without Isaac.

Placing both hands behind his back, he stared down at the street below him. People hurried from place to place, unaware that they were probably constantly being watched. They looked like a bunch of little worker ants, going about their days. A sign outside of a convenience store below boasted the best soft serve frozen yogurt in town. Maybe he'd get some before heading to the casino.

That used to be him. He'd been a substitute teacher for a local alternative high school before his uncle had ripped him from that world and placed him here. Things had changed so much over the last six months and as much as he wished he could go back, he knew he was in the right place.

The door to the conference room opened and he turned to find Isaac entering, a stack of folders in his arm. He flashed Bart a smile and gestured toward the conference table. "Take a seat." Isaac was the epitome of a slick CEO. His black hair was perfectly cut and styled without a single hair out of place. His strong jaw didn't need any facial hair to make him look intimidating. And his steel blue eyes could hold any opponent in their place. It wasn't any wonder his uncle had hired him.

Bart strode toward the table and returned to his chair. Isaac sat in his usual place at the head. He pushed the folders across the table. "I just got these on my desk yesterday. Care to explain?" His gaze was steady, unnerving even, but not unhappy.

Leaning forward, Bart grabbed the folders and flipped the top one open. A quick cursory glance gave him all the information he needed. "Those are the contracts for the sale of the casinos. We discussed that they were to be sold months ago. This shouldn't be a surprise."

Isaac shook his head. "The sale, no. But the proceeds of the sale, yes. You failed to mention that the proceeds were in part going to Maple Gardens Assisted Living."

Bart stilled. Had he done something wrong? He didn't think charitable donations had to be approved. "Is that unacceptable?"

Isaac steepled his fingers in front of him and brought them to his chin. "No. On the contrary, it was very generous of you to think of them—us. When your uncle gifted me that facility, I was as surprised as any. But I assumed it was because he had a special place in his heart for me—and my mother."

"How is Millie doing?"

A slow smile tugged at his lips. "You're getting off subject. The reason I wanted to call you in here was to give you my thanks for your generosity. The amount of money you're giving Maple Gardens would pay for your uncle's treatment ten times over."

"Well, you're welcome. I know you'll do better things with it."

"I want you to know that we will not be charging you or your uncle for his care from this point forward."

Bart straightened in his seat. "That's not necessary. He has more than enough income to—"

Isaac held up his hand. "It's done."

Folding his arms tight against his chest, Bart huffed. "Well, if this is how you're going to react to that donation, you might not be thrilled with what I have planned next."

Isaac arched a brow but didn't say a word.

"My uncle has more money and income than anyone in their right mind knows what to do with. There is no way I'd be able to spend a tenth of it even if I lived for twenty lifetimes. As discussed, I'm keeping the first casino he bought. But I will be giving all profits from that place to charity as well. Don't be surprised if a portion of that money finds its way to Maple Gardens. Those residents need it more."

Isaac chuckled and shook his head. "You know what I think? I think your uncle knew what he was doing when he left all of this to you," he gestured around them. "You're a good man, Bart, and I look forward to working with you." Isaac stood and held out his hand, offering it to Bart.

Bart stared at it for a moment before he accepted it. "Thanks Isaac. I look forward to working with you, too."

Chapter Three

Izzie ducked into the convenience store where she worked and hurried around the cashier's counter. She glanced at the clock, her face red as her supervisor appeared from the back office. Dang it.

Mr. Perry folded his arms, shaking his head. "You can't keep being late, Isobel. I have a business to run."

Her eyes darted away as she placed her magazine on the counter, grabbed her apron and put it over her head. "I'm so sorry, Mr. Perry. I had to visit with my mother this morning then I got stopped by a train. And—" She shook her head. Excuses had never gotten her sympathy before. "It won't happen again."

The look on his face seemed to say he didn't have much faith in that promise. He shook his head and returned to the back office. Luckily there wasn't anyone in the store. On days when she was late and there was a line, he really got upset. Luckily, he hadn't fired her yet.

Izzie leaned against the back counter and placed her hands in her apron pockets. She really should start looking for another job. This place barely helped her pay her rent.

And now with the bills for her mother's care piling up, she didn't know what she was going to do. She'd already sold too many of her belongings.

Her chest tightened. The most recent one sliced through her the sharpest. The guitar her grandmother had given her had been the one thing that had kept her sane. But sacrifices had to be made. She was an only child and no one was around to help out.

She looked up at the ceiling, fighting the emotion that always burned behind her eyes when she started getting down on herself. She'd make it out alright. She always did. Izzie glanced back to where Mr. Perry was probably hard at work balancing the till. Her gaze slipped over to the newspaper and she picked it up. There was another estate sale this upcoming weekend. How had she missed it?

Izzie pulled out a pen and circled the classified listing a few times. The bell above the glass door jingled. Without looking up, she murmured. "Welcome to Perry's Convenience Shop. Let me know if I can get you anything." The guest shuffled through the store, not speaking. Typical.

She chewed on the back of her pen and skimmed the classifieds once more. If she'd missed one, she might have missed another.

A cup of frozen soft-serve slid on the counter toward her.

Izzie lifted her gaze and froze, coming face to face with *him*.

He wore the most infuriatingly confident smile on his face. "Hello again."

She straightened, placing both hands on her hips. "Are you *following* me?"

His brows lifted and he chuckled. "I had business across the street. I saw the sign. Am I not permitted to enjoy the best soft-serve frozen yogurt in Atlanta?" He nudged the cup filled with white ice cream toward her again.

Her focus shifted to the cup and she scoffed. "You picked vanilla? You realize we have like six flavors, right? You didn't even get any toppings."

Bart shrugged. "Maybe I appreciate plain."

Her brows creased. Something about his statement rubbed her the wrong way but she didn't have the ability to dissect the reasons at the moment. She shook her head and placed the ice cream on the small scale beside the cash register. "It will be six-eighty-three."

He handed her a ten from his wallet. "Keep the change."

Izzie shook her head. "I can't. It will ruin the balance in the till."

Bart's smile lifted at one side. "You're not allowed to pocket the change?"

Her face burned red and she shoved the change across the counter. "*No*. I'm not a waitress. I'm a cashier."

His eyes didn't leave her face, making her whole body tense up. The blood coursing through her veins hummed with a strange kind of energy.

She shifted and gestured toward his ice cream. "Enjoy, come again."

"Oh, I will." He grabbed the cup and saluted her with his spoon.

Her eyes widened. She hadn't meant to say that. She didn't want him to come again. She didn't want him to come back ever. Her teeth clenched, fighting the urge to call out to him and inform him of that fact. He wasn't a good guy, as much as he probably *thought* he was. She knew better. She'd seen evidence with her own eyes.

Her gaze followed him as he headed out the door without looking back at her. Great. Now he knew where she worked. He also knew where her mother stayed. Something inside her said this wouldn't be the last time she'd be seeing him and that notion infuriated her.

"Wait. Hold up. He showed up at your *work*?" Olivia yanked Izzie to a stop causing a sharp pain to shoot through her arm.

Izzie yelped, rubbing where her arm felt like it had nearly been pulled from its socket. She shot Olivia a disgruntled look.

"Sorry," her friend murmured, chagrined. "But seriously. You can't leave it at that. Bartholomew, billionaire, just showed up at your work? Was he stalking you or something? I mean he's still fairly new so I haven't gotten to know him very well over at Maple Gardens. But he's super hot and—"

"Olivia," Izzie laughed. "You're not even letting me get a word in edgewise." They wandered through the living room of the first house on her list, looking through jewelry boxes and old trinkets. "First of all, I have no idea if he was stalking me. He *said* he was just in the area." She fought the urge to roll her eyes. "But more importantly, it doesn't matter that he's hot. I'd be very happy if I never saw him again."

"That's too bad."

Her eyes shot open, and she jumped. Both she and Olivia spun around to look up into a pair of chocolate eyes. Why oh why did this keep happening to her? She clapped her hand over her mouth, praying her face wasn't as red as it felt. How much had he heard?

That was a stupid question. He'd probably heard the

worst of it. Based on the smirk he was sporting, he was thrilled he had.

Izzie turned around and nudged Olivia's shoulder with her own. "You have to get me out of here," she muttered.

Her friend snorted. "Are you kidding? This is the most exciting thing that has happened to me since I can't remember when."

"*Olivia*!" she hissed.

Her friend spun around and faced Bart, holding out her hand. "Hi, I'm Olivia. Izzie's friend."

Izzie refused to turn around. This was embarrassing. More than that, it was mortifying. She dug through a pile of heirlooms on the table in front of her, if only to keep her hands busy. Clearly pretending to be engaged in something other than Bart did nothing to dissuade him from sticking around.

His warm as honey voice floated around her, giving her goosebumps. "Hello, Olivia. You work at Maple Gardens? Perhaps you can explain to me why my presence irks your friend so much."

Olivia laughed obnoxiously loud. "It might have some-thing to do with the fact that you own the—"

Izzie elbowed Olivia with her elbow, receiving a sharp look and a grunt from her friend. Bart raised a brow, his gaze dipping to where Olivia rubbed her side. She smiled but it resembled a painful grimace more than anything else. "Actually, I haven't a clue. Sometimes she's just mean." Olivia gave Izzie a pointed look.

Izzie's blush deepened despite her best efforts to look more nonchalant about this whole weird situation she found herself in. She folded her arms and met Bart's gaze. "I don't think you can talk yourself out of this one. I don't know how you did it, but I *know* you followed me here. Are you spying on me?"

How was he so at ease? He exuded confidence despite being caught following her around town. There had to be something wrong with him.

Bart leaned toward her and she sucked in a breath as he reached for a vase that was on the table beside her. His arm brushed against hers, sending a fresh wave of goosebumps rising along her skin. She rubbed at them vigorously, her features darkening.

He turned the vase over in both his hands and flashed her a smile fit for the cover of GQ magazine. "Maybe I like collecting old things, too."

Izzie's eyes narrowed. "Do you actually expect me to believe that?"

Olivia jumped in before he could comment. "I believe you."

Bart smiled at her friend this time and Izzie's stomach tightened.

Olivia tucked a strand of hair behind her ear and seemed to lean closer to Bart. "It's so sweet of you to come visit your uncle so much. Have the two of you always been close?"

Leave it to Olivia to flirt up a storm with the devil incarnate. Izzie edged away from them as Bart launched into a conversation with her best friend. If Olivia wanted to flirt with a guy who didn't have any morals, that was her decision. Izzie wouldn't step in her way.

But as she put more distance between herself and the two budding love birds, she couldn't rid herself of that strange sick feeling in her stomach. The way they were talking, the way Olivia brushed her hand up and down his upper arm was making her feel almost sick to her stomach.

It was probably something she'd eaten earlier in the day. She needed to get Bart out of her head. She was here for one thing and one thing only—to see if the deceased was in possession of her mother's jade necklace.

There had to be more jewelry around here somewhere. This estate had boasted several pieces of fine jewelry on the listing. But all she was seeing were cheap baubles. There were brooches and gaudy earrings, too but no necklace pieces.

Just another let down.

Izzie didn't even know if she wanted to bother going to the other estate sale she'd circled in the paper. And based on the way Olivia had abandoned her to chat with Bart, it looked like Izzie would be flying solo at this point.

She shot a look over where she'd left Olivia, finding them gone. Izzie stiffened and scanned the room. Where had they gone? This wasn't like Olivia. Sure, she'd flirt like no one's business. But she wouldn't just abandon her friend.

Izzie wandered through the room toward the kitchen where there was more set up. Neither of the people she was looking for were there. Izzie's brows furrowed until she saw the two of them chatting on the back porch.

This visit had been a bust. But Olivia had driven them, and if she wanted to leave, she'd have to go interrupt the conversation they were having.

Izzie took a deep breath, steeling herself for the very likely possibility that Bart would pull her into another humiliating conversation. It was fine. She'd drag Olivia out to the car, they'd make one quick stop at the next place and then Olivia could text Bart and the two of them would inevitably go on a date. That was just the way things would work out.

So why was there still this strange nausea rolling through her stomach? She didn't even like Bart. Maybe it was simply the fact that she knew and loved Olivia. She couldn't let her friend be dragged down by the likes of Bartholomew Brown.

Izzie stepped out onto the back porch just as Olivia got a phone call. Bart glanced at Izzie, smiling again. Ergh, that infuriating smile that could make anyone's knees go weak. It was a weapon and it should be illegal for him to use it.

Olivia hung up her phone, her eyes darting to Izzie. The look on her face said it all.

Uh oh.

Chapter Four

Bart glanced from Olivia to Izzie and back.

"I'm so sorry, Izzie. But I have to go into work. I don't even have time to run home and change. A girl called in sick and they're already understaffed."

"Wait, you can't even take me home?"

"Maybe you can get an Uber? Or you could drop me off at work and borrow my car. I'm totally okay with that."

Izzie sighed. "It's fine. I'll just skip the next one."

"Are you sure? Because I feel awful. I know I promised we'd get to both of them but—"

"I can take you," Bart jumped in, only realizing it when both woman turned to gape at him. He cleared his throat. "I mean, wherever you need to go, I'm not busy."

"Of course you're not," Izzie muttered.

Olivia's eyes widened and her smile broadened. "Really? That's so sweet of you. Isn't that sweet, Izzie?"

There was zero pleasure emanating from Izzie's body language. She gave her friend a look that clearly said she didn't want anything to do with him. And for some reason that made him want to help her even more. He knew exactly where she wanted to go. In fact, he had just come from there.

If Izzie were to borrow Olivia's car and do what her friend suggested, she would end up going an hour out of her way just to get back to this side of town. It wasn't a logical choice. But he had his Maserati here and he was itching to find out what Olivia had nearly admitted when he'd walked in on their conversation.

Izzie heaved an exaggerated sigh. "You don't even know where I want to go. How can you make an offer like that?"

Bart shrugged. "Maybe I'm just a good guy."

She snorted.

Olivia crossed the distance between herself and Izzie. "I'll make this up to you," she murmured. "I promise." She glanced over her shoulder at Bart. "It was nice meeting you, Bart." Then she darted inside and disappeared, leaving him alone with Izzie.

They stood in awkward silence until he finally broke it. "Well? Aren't you going to tell me where we're going?"

Izzie threw up her hands and went inside, forcing him to follow.

"I'm not falling for your good-guy act," she bit out as she wove through the display tables.

He jogged to keep up with her. "Who says it's an act?"

She huffed but didn't say anything.

He reached out and grasped her wrist, tugging her to a stop. "Did I do something to offend you?" Bart stared into her eyes, searching for something he wasn't sure he'd find. "Because it seems like from the second we met, you have absolutely despised me."

Her gaze locked onto his for only a moment before she dragged them away and wouldn't meet his eyes.

"I don't believe you're this angry all the time."

Izzie's focus shot back to meet his and she yanked her wrist from his grasp. "I'm *not* angry."

Bart chuckled. "You could have fooled me." He ran a hand through his hair. "Maybe we got off on the wrong foot."

"I don't think so." She turned to start walking away once more.

Letting out a groan, Bart followed her through the front door and down the sidewalk toward the street. She paused in front of his car and shot him a disgusted look. "Seriously? You brought *that*?" She gestured toward his cherry-red Maserati.

"What? It's my car."

Izzie rolled her eyes, folding her arms as she waited for him to unlock it. "Do you *know* how many people could be fed if the money that paid for that car was given to a food bank? Or how many bills would get paid? You pretend to be this wonderful human being but you drive around in a car that would pay for—" she cut herself off and shook her head. "You know what? No. It's none of my business what you spend your money on. I'm not going to let you bring me down."

"*Me*?" The word came out in more of a bark of laughter than anything else. "What did I ever do to you?"

She sliced her hand through the air. "Just unlock the door so we can get this over with." She shook her head again, muttering, "I should have just driven my car."

Normally he wouldn't have stuck around this long. Izzie was obviously dealing with some personal issues. But there was something about her that he couldn't let go. He'd felt it like an electrical current between the two of them when they'd first met. Something had drawn him to her and he couldn't get her out of his head.

The ride to the next estate sale was about twenty minutes if traffic agreed with them. Maybe he'd be able to redeem himself from whatever he'd said or done to upset her so much.

He lifted the key fob in his hand toward the car and clicked to unlock and start it. She climbed inside and shut the door before he had a chance to do it for her.

Bart got behind the wheel, put the car into drive and started down the road. When he peeked at her out of the corner of his eye, he was surprised to find her gaping at him. The look on her face was unnerving at best. "*What*?"

Izzie threw her hands in the air. "*Seriously*? How did you know where we're going?" She held up both hands and shook her head vigorously. "Nope. Stop the car."

He glanced at her again. "What?"

"I said *stop the car*," she practically screeched it, startling him. He swerved to the shoulder of the road and put the car into park.

"What is your problem?" He turned to face her.

"My problem? What's your problem? You're stalking me. Deny it all you want, but I know what's going on. First Maple Gardens. Then my work. Now you know what I'm doing and where I'm going to be over the weekend? This is just too much. I'm not going to be part of some Dateline special." She reached for the door handle and yanked but it didn't do anything. She yanked a second time and a third, her movements becoming more erratic. "Let me out!"

He just stared at her, wide-eyed. "Fine!"

Izzie froze.

"I knew you were going to be here because I saw it circled on the newspaper you were reading. Bad idea. I get it."

Izzie settled back in her seat. "I knew it," she muttered. "You know that's creepy, right?"

He rubbed his jaw. "I do *now*."

She stared out the window, a sullen look on her face. "Did you ever consider simply asking for my number?"

"And you would have given it to me?"

"No," she scoffed rather quickly. She peeked at him and the corners of her mouth twitched. "No," she repeated. "Because you're not my type."

A fleeting disappointment stirred in his midsection. What was he supposed to say to that? Argue with her? Tell her she should give him a chance? It was clear she had already made her judgments about him and he had no choice but to accept them.

Unless he didn't.

He had twenty minutes to figure her out.

Bart cleared his throat. "Well, I don't have anywhere to go today, and you do. So I'll take you to that other estate sale and we can see where things go from there."

"We'll go to that other estate sale, and then we'll go our separate ways." She gave him a pointed look. "And you'll stop stalking me."

A rumbled chuckle bounced around his chest. "I wasn't *stalking you*. But if it would make you feel better, then sure. Let's go with that." He gestured to the road. "Do I have your permission to start driving now?"

She nodded, folding her arms across her chest. They drove in silence for a few minutes. He wanted the dust to settle before he even attempted to make small chat. Isobel Davis had made it perfectly clear she didn't trust easy. Or maybe it was just him. Which begged the question, what could she possibly have against him?

Passing trees changed to businesses as they headed into

the city. He'd looked the place up online. It was a nice place, one he could have seen his uncle staying in if his memory hadn't failed him.

Bart cleared his throat and she glanced at him. "What?"

"Why are you going to estate sales?"

She huffed. "I don't see why that's any business of yours."

He shook his head. "I don't know what you have against me, but be forewarned that your opinion will change."

Izzie snorted. "This isn't something you can change."

"So you *do* have something against me."

Her face burned scarlet and she twisted to look out the window. "No." Her tone didn't sound convincing.

Shrugging off his burning curiosity, he glanced at her. "So why are you going to estate sales? Are you a collector?"

She shook her head. "Do I look like someone with the money to be able to collect things of value?" The bite in her voice softened as she expelled a breath. "Sorry." Izzie glanced at him, facing forward again. She tucked a loose strand of red hair behind her ear. "I'm looking for something my mother lost a long time ago."

"Sounds like there's a story there."

Izzie's scowl returned. "Just because I'm letting you take me to this estate sale doesn't mean we're going to be best friends."

"Why not?"

She gaped at him and he laughed again. She threw her hands in the air. "Why would you want to?"

He considered her for a moment then swiveled his attention back to the road. Thrumming his fingers on the steering wheel, he considered his words carefully. She wasn't impressed by him or what she could probably have googled. She didn't want to be his friend for whatever reason. But he was far too intrigued with her to let her just walk out of his life. A wry smile touched his lips. "Because anyone who would read Jane Austen to my uncle is someone I want to be friends with."

Her mouth snapped closed and her eyes softened. Or maybe that was just his imagination. Izzie turned her attention to the road before them, having gone quiet. They made it about five miles before she spoke again. "With all due respect, you don't seem like the type who makes friends with people like me."

The words hit him like a splash of cold water. "People like you? What is that supposed to mean?" He shot her a confused look.

Her cheeks reddened again and she fiddled with her hair. "You know. Like me."

He snorted. "No, I don't know. What are you talking about?"

Her next statement was tossed at him in exasperation. "You know. Plain. Bookish. Poor." The last word was muttered under her breath but he caught it. "My apartment complex is right outside your casino. I've seen you come and go from that place with several different women. In fact I don't think I've seen the same women twice." She fidgeted in her seat, avoiding looking straight at him.

His lips quirked into a smirk. "So *you've* been spying on *me*."

Chapter Five

A horrible taste rose into Izzie's throat. How on earth had he twisted this conversation and stolen all the power so quickly? The heat from her cheeks could probably cook the egg on her face. She squirmed in her seat, risking a glance in his direction.

He was openly grinning at her. The nerve!

"I am not spying on you. You're flaunting the fact that you spend the evening with a different girl on your arm every single weekend." Okay so that accusation did nothing to help her. She blew out a frustrated breath. "The point is, I don't have any interest in a guy like you and you don't have any interest in a girl like me—based on your current preferences. So there's no point in us even entertaining the idea of a friendship. We're like oil and vinegar."

"Isn't oil and vinegar like some kind of fancy salad dressing?"

Izzie released a groan. "Just drop it, will you?"

He pulled to a stop in front of an old house, shut off the engine and faced her. "All of what you just said only makes me want to be friends with you more."

The strangled sound that came from her lips as she darted from the car probably made her seem a little more than crazy. She stalked toward the house, ignoring the sound of his footsteps as he followed her.

Bart jogged beside her to catch up. "You still didn't answer my question."

She shot him an irritated look. "What question?"

"The thing your mother lost. What was it? Maybe I can help."

Izzie huffed. "No thank you."

He darted in front of her, making her almost bump into him. His brown puppy-dog eyes seemed to plead with her. She'd always been a sucker for that sort of thing.

Izzie rolled her eyes and shoved past him as she made her way into the old brick building. "Fine."

Bart hurried to catch up to her. "Great. So what are we looking for?"

"It's a jade necklace. The stone is the shape of a heart and there's an inscription on the back."

"Got it." Somehow, he'd managed to make it to the door before her. He pushed it open, gesturing for her to enter first.

Izzie's eyes narrowed. Bart was this wealthy casino owner who could have his pick of anyone and here he was on a weekend holding open the door for her. Something didn't feel right. People in his station didn't just do that sort of thing. But he was being far too persistent and she hadn't been able to shake him off yet. She might as well accept his help until they found the necklace and *then* maybe he'd leave her alone.

The foyer had tall ceilings that stretched at least fifteen feet in the air. A fancy light fixture hung overhead, filling the already open entryway with light. From the outside, the building had looked old, but well-maintained. It was located in the historical district. But on the inside of the building, it had been remodeled. The owners had managed to keep the feel of an older home with all new paint, flooring, and updated panes in the windows. The foyer opened on the left to a study and on the right to a parlor. Both rooms were filled with people looking through the items for sale.

Izzie moved toward the parlor first, praying Bart would take a hint and go in the opposite direction. Instead, he followed her. Dang it.

She stopped at a table near the front window and picked up a vase, turning it over in her hand. The crystal winked at her, hit by the sunlight streaming into the house. Bart brushed past her, his arm grazing hers. Goosebumps sprouted on her arms.

Izzie peeked over her shoulder as he floated from display to display. He didn't pick anything up, but kept his hands clasped behind his back as he peered at each item. Once she was done in the parlor, she moved into the study. Immediately her eyes were drawn to a guitar that perched on a stand in the corner.

Her heart fluttered. It was beautiful. The red wood grain seemed to glow beneath the lacquer finish. Her fingers itched to glide along the strings that had been pulled taut.

"Do you play?" Bart's warm breath grazed against the sensitive skin at her neck sending a fresh wave of chills down her back.

She jumped then stepped away from him, putting as much distance as she could. Izzie shrugged, dragging her gaze away from the instrument. "A little."

Bart moved past her. He picked up the guitar by its neck and turned it. "It's a Gibson. Is that good?"

Izzie moved over to the desk, setting her sights on an old-fashioned ink well. "Like any brand, Gibson makes both high end and starter guitars."

Bart moved toward her and shoved the guitar at her with more force than necessary. "Is this one high end?"

She gasped, snatching the delicate instrument from his hands. "You can't *do* that. Yes. This one is very nice." Izzie turned the instrument over in her hands, marveling at the cool, smooth finish. Her fingers brushed against the strings, filling the room with a soft twang.

This one was so much finer than the one she'd sold to pay for her mother's care. It was probably too expensive just to hold in her hand, but oh, did she dream of owning something like this one day.

"You should get it." Bart's words dragged her back to reality.

She started, her eyes lifting to meet his. Shaking her head vehemently, she hurried across the room. She placed it on its stand with care. "It's gorgeous," she murmured reverently. "But it's too expensive."

Izzie turned to find Bart standing directly behind her. She sucked in a sharp breath and shoved past him. "You really shouldn't sneak up on people like that." There were no pieces of jewelry in the study. She'd have to track down whoever was in charge before she could leave and get away from Bart.

Thirty minutes of digging through jewelry left her empty-handed. Her hands smelled like the metal she'd been handling. Izzie returned a box filled with different pieces to the top of a dresser and heaved a disappointed sigh. Her whole Saturday had been a big mess. She'd be visiting her mother tomorrow with nothing but bad news.

Bart had stopped following her at some point. He could

be anywhere in the building by now. Heck, he could have left her there and she'd have to call an Uber. A tiny part of her admitted that might have been the best thing that could have happened to her. But competing with that thought was a much stronger one that would be disappointed to discover he didn't even bother to tell her he was leaving.

She wandered through the upstairs of the house, poking her head into several bedrooms until she found him in a library. The room was probably supposed to be storage, but the owner had installed several shelves that filled the walls up to the high ceilings.

Bart's back faced her and his head was stooped. He had put all his weight on one foot. His left arm moved and the sound of rustling paper filled the small room as he turned the page. She stepped into the doorway and leaned her shoulder against the doorjamb. "Find anything interesting?"

He jumped and glanced over his shoulder at her before turning and showing her a book that looked to be at least twice her age if not older. "This is a first edition of Sense and Sensibility."

Her eyes rounded and she moved the few feet into the room. She peered at the old book, the pages yellowed with age. The hard cover was a light brown, golden color. Bart shifted, flipping the book to the cover page and angling it so she could get a clear view of it. "See?"

Izzie's gaze bounced to meet his, whispering, "How much do you think its worth?"

He turned the book over in his hands, flipping through the pages then snapped it closed. "I've seen one of these before. If had to guess, I'd say about six thousand."

"*Six thousand?*" She shrieked in a whisper. Izzie grabbed

ahold of him, turning him toward the shelves and giving him a push. "Put it back. *Now.*"

Bart dragged his feet, a crooked smile on his lips. "Why?"

Her head reared back. Did he just ask her that? "That book is worth more than my car, that's why. I'm not going to be party to you doing something stupid with it." She backed away, making her way toward the door. "I'm ready to go. You take care of that and meet me out at the car."

He was still examining the book when she made her way down the hall toward the stairs. Whoever had lived in this home had been in the upper class. It was somewhat surprising that she hadn't found any jewelry resembling the necklace she was after. It was back to the drawing board. The necklace hadn't been in any of the local pawn shops. Nor had any of the local jewelers seen it. These estate sales and auctions were her last shot.

She didn't allow herself to become distracted as she headed toward Bart's car. Once outside, she stopped to stare at his Maserati. Bart's reaction to the expensive book had been disappointing. No, disappointing was the wrong word. It had been unexpected, sure. Maybe it was the way he'd carelessly handled the book. She held books much the same way. It was just the way he held a book that cost so much.

Izzie sighed, moving onward and toward his car. She climbed inside and waited in the passenger seat, her patience wearing thin. Today had started with so much hope. She'd had a feeling that something good would happen. How wrong she'd been.

Now, she sat in the car of the man she loathed with nothing to show for it.

Bart appeared from the house and wandered down the

sidewalk toward the street where he'd parked. She kept tabs on him out of the corner of her eye but did her best to keep her focus elsewhere. He walked around the car and climbed in. Before he started the car, he dropped something heavy into her lap.

Izzie jumped and looked down. A quiet curse left her throat as she faced him. "Bart! What's this?"

He started the car, glancing at her. "Sense and Sensibility."

"I know *that*. What on earth are you doing with it?" Her gaze swung toward the house and back to him. She leaned forward and lowered her voice. "Did you steal it?"

His warm chuckle sent waves of electrical pulses through her body. If she didn't dislike him so much that sort of laugh would be enough to make her heart skip a beat. Bart moved closer to her and lowered his voice to the same conspiratorial tone. "I recently came into some money and I don't mind spending it on my friends."

Her mouth dropped open. He couldn't be suggesting...

"I hope it brings you some semblance of pleasure, Izzie." He shifted back into his seat and pulled away from the house, leaving her speechlessly holding a six thousand dollar book.

38

Chapter Six

Though the book was definitely worth six thousand dollars, the people inside that house didn't know what they could get for it. He'd only spent half the amount they might have gotten for it at auction. But Bart wasn't about to tell Izzie that.

He bit back a smile as he glanced at her out of the corner of his eye. She stared at the book in her hands, holding it almost reverently. She deserved that book. He could tell just by the way she softly traced the title with her hands. Too many people didn't value literature.

Izzie wasn't one of them.

Warmth filled his chest as he continued driving. He turned on the radio, pushing the silence that had filled the car aside. The drive toward her apartment went too fast for his liking. When he pulled into the parking lot and shut off the car, she jumped.

Her eyes narrowed. "How did you know I live here?"

"Easy, Izzie. You said you live at the apartment complex right beside my casino."

"But you own several."

"Not anymore. This is the only one I've stepped foot in for the last several weeks."

Her brows furrowed with confusion. She shook her head and held out the book to him. "I can't accept this."

His gaze dipped to the book then bounced up to meet hers. "Sorry?"

She emphasized her refusal by lifting and holding it out to him again. "It's very generous of you, þut I can't in good conscience accept this. It's too much money."

"It wasn't really that much."

Izzie's laugh held a manic tone to it. "Do you even hear yourself? I could sell this book to pay for my mom's treatment at the retirement home. I could sell it to pay for my rent. I could pay bills and buy groceries—"

He placed a finger against the binding and pushed the book toward her. "But you wouldn't."

"You don't know that." The tone of her voice held a little bite, but not as much as before. "You can't just throw money at people and expect them to like you."

A wry smile touched his lips. "I can't?"

Izzie shook her head vehemently. "Of course you can't. Money can buy you a lot of stuff, but it can't buy that."

He glanced at the book once more. "I gave you that book, Izzie. It wasn't conditional. You don't have to be my friend or spend time with me. Heck, I'm not even asking you out on a date. It was an honest to goodness peace offering."

Her argument was wavering. All he had to do was tip it over the edge. "I want you to have it. Everyone deserves nice things."

Something in her countenance darkened. "Having nice things isn't a privilege, Bart. Not everyone is handed everything on a silver spoon. Some people have to make sacrifices that slice through them like a knife. I really appreciate it, but I can't and won't accept this." She reached for the handle and pushed the door open. Once she was outside, she placed the book on the seat. "Thanks for the ride, Bart."

His eyes followed her as she hurried across the parking lot, weaving between cars and pausing to let a bicyclist pass. Bart's focus remained on the door of the complex long after she'd disappeared within its confines.

Then he stared at the book that sat a bit forlornly beside him. Sure, he could take the book home and add it to his collection. He didn't have *Sense and Sensibility*. But something felt wrong about that. He'd bought it with Izzie in mind. She needed to have it. She deserved it.

A frown filled his face. What was it with people and not willingly accepting gifts? Yes, they were still practically strangers, but he'd spent almost the whole afternoon with her. He'd like to think he'd learned a little more than a stranger would know.

Izzie could play the guitar but she was shy about playing. She loved to read classics to her mother—lots of Jane Austin. She was very distrustful—*very*. And she had insecurities with money.

At one point he had been in the same boat. It wasn't until he signed the documents to accept the inheritance his uncle had left him that the reality had set in. He had more money than he'd be able to spend in ten lifetimes. Twenty lifetimes, even.

Bart heaved a sigh and put his car into drive. He'd figure her out eventually. Izzie was different which made her all the more interesting. She couldn't hide from him for long. Eventually he got to the root of what made people tick. The same would happen with Izzie. He just had to be patient.

Bart's focus shifted toward the entrance of the gardens each time an orderly and a resident passed by or wandered down the trail. He didn't know anything about Izzie's schedule so predicting when she'd arrive at Maple Gardens to visit her mother was an improbability.

He should have been at meetings today, but he'd appointed someone to attend in his stead just so he could see her reaction when she found out what he'd done. The orderly that wandered into the gardens offered him and Lawrence a smile before turning down a path in a different direction.

Bart heaved a sigh and turned back to the book he was reading. "I can't believe I didn't think to read to you, Uncle Larry. I don't know if you liked reading before your stroke, but this is a great way to keep the conversation going, don't you think?"

As per usual, his uncle didn't move. His mouth hung open slightly and his eyes stared off into an abyss where Bart wasn't allowed to go. He sighed again. Getting his uncle to be even a fraction more alert these days was getting harder and harder.

Izzie had accomplished it—she'd been a natural. Unless it was her mother who had that effect on his uncle. He glanced up at Lawrence. "Should we go see if Margaret is available today?"

Nothing.

Bart scratched his cheek, his brows furrowed. There was just something about Izzie. He couldn't explain it. Maybe it was that she was down to earth. Or how she cared about her mother. And yes, the way she didn't fawn over him was admittedly refreshing. Ever since he received his inheritance from his uncle, people only saw dollar signs. He wasn't Bart Brown. He was Bartholomew Brown, nephew of billionaire real estate mogul—Lawrence Travis.

But with Izzie, it was different. She didn't want him to spend his money on her or take her to fancy restaurants. And she'd gotten over the initial dislike of him—at least it appeared that way. A smile touched his lips as he thought back to the way she'd stared at him when he'd given her that book. He couldn't wait to see her reaction regarding his new plans with the book.

Motion caught his attention again and his heart leapt into his throat. Izzie pushed the wheelchair carrying her mother toward them. Margaret waved happily but Izzie's expression bordered on grim. Or was she nervous? Either way, she didn't look pleased to see him.

His excitement waned momentarily. Bart snapped his book closed and rose to meet them. His focus dipped to Margaret. "Good morning. How are you doing?"

Izzie's mother beamed at him. "Simply marvelous. It's wonderful to see you again, Bart. I'm sure Lawrence is happy to have visitors." She placed her hands on the wheelchair and inched closer to his uncle, chatting happily with him.

He took a step toward Izzie, sidling next to her and folded his arms. "How was the rest of your weekend?"

She seemed stiff. "Fine."

"Anything else exciting happen?"

Izzie shot him a look out of the corner of her eye. "No. I worked. What about you? Did you find anyone to give that book to?"

The corners of his mouth twitched. "Actually, I realized there was someone who would appreciate that book as much as you. Maybe more."

Something flickered in her expression. He couldn't be certain if it was disappointment or something else. Was she having second thoughts about refusing to accept the gift he'd offered? Maybe he should give her another chance to accept it.

Nah. The way her body stood rigid like she wanted nothing more than to be rid of him. There would be no way for him to convince her to take the book. He'd just have to come up with another way to get her to like him.

He moved away from her, toward the bench where he'd been sitting. "Margaret, your daughter tells me you enjoy reading the classics."

"*Bart*—" Izzie's voice bordered on accusatory.

Reaching into a satchel that he'd put on the ground next to his feet, he retrieved the book he'd purchased at that estate sale. "I thought you might like to have this." He held out the hardcover book.

Margaret reached for it reverently. "It's lovely." Her hand traced over the cover before she flipped open the book and read the title. A smile lit her face like the morning sun that had crested the horizon a few hours ago. "*Sense and Sensibility*?"

"Bart you don't have to—" Izzie stepped toward them but stopped when her mother shot her a confused look.

"What's the matter, dear?" She looked down at the book again. "Isn't it wonderful? I have never seen such a beautiful printing."

"Yes, it's beautiful, mom."

Margaret turned toward Uncle Larry and showed him the book, flipping through the pages.

Bart stood, grabbing the strap to his satchel and placing it on his shoulder. He almost dreaded to meet Izzie's expression. But when he did, he was surprised to find it void of the irritation he'd expected.

Her eyes flicked from her mother to him and back.

"You okay?" He spoke quietly as he stood beside her once more. "I just figured I didn't have a use for that book and since you didn't want—"

She hugged herself, rubbing her hands up and down her arms. "You were very generous to think of her. I know she'll cherish that book." Izzie pressed her lips together and slowly lifted her gaze to meet his again. "Thank you."

Bart tilted his head, his eyes drilling into hers. "So it is okay to spend that kind of money on your mother but it isn't okay for me to do the exact same thing for you?"

Her cheeks flushed. "It's different and you know it."

He laughed. "How so? Please enlighten me."

Izzie's features reddened further and she shifted, moving a fraction from him. "Because you're *you* and I'm —me."

Bart laughed again. "That doesn't make a lick of sense."

She blew out an exasperated breath. "Because if you give that book to my mother, you're not expecting her to go on a date with you or—" Izzie looked away.

He wagged his eyebrows. "Who says?"

Her disbelieving gaze shot to meet his, causing another bout of laughter to escape his chest. "Don't worry, Izzie. I'm not interested in dating your mother. Like I said on Saturday, that book was meant to be a gift. Whether it was for you or your mother it didn't matter to me. I just wanted to do something nice for the people who are spending time with my uncle." He adjusted the strap on his shoulder and flashed her a smile. "Maybe I'll see you around."

Chapter Seven

Izzie watched Bart turn on his heel and head toward the side of the building where he'd get access to the parking lot. Her mouth had dropped open. Was it possible she'd misjudged him?

She shook her head. People could be nice or pretend to be so and still be a bad person in other ways. Bart still owned casinos that promoted gambling, drinking, and destroying one's livelihood. Anyone who could condone such habits wasn't someone she wanted to spend her time with.

But as he disappeared from view she couldn't be so sure. Okay, yes, he'd stepped over the line when he'd planned a way to bump into her. But then he'd been willing take extra time out of his day to help her when she'd been nothing but cold to him.

Now as she glanced at her mother holding that book with a fresh excitement in her eyes that Izzie hadn't seen in a long time, she felt conflicted. Izzie sat on the bench beside her mother's wheelchair and smiled at her as she chatted to both Lawrence and her daughter over the book she held.

She hadn't mentioned even once that the book was a first edition. She didn't seem to care. Margaret was just thrilled to have a beautiful book she could read.

Inwardly, Izzie stifled a groan. She was going to have to figure out a way to thank him appropriately. Saying a verbal thanks wasn't enough for what he'd done. But what could she do for a millionaire? Or was he a billionaire? It wasn't like she could just make a batch of cookies. He probably had a maid for that sort of thing. He had money so buying him a gift was out of the question.

She sat back on the bench and ran a hand through her hair. Great. She'd have to be friends with the guy. Why did simply thinking about doing so fill her with both a great deal of trepidation and excitement at the same time?

His handsome face flashed in her mind and her stomach flipped over. Maybe she'd get lucky and they wouldn't bump into each other again for a long time. Then she would be able to get her head on straight. There had to be a way to be friends with someone who didn't share the same values with her.

"Izzie. I think this is for you."

She jumped and her focus landed on her mother. Margaret held out an envelope with Izzie's name scrawled over the front of it. Izzie reached for the envelope, a mixture of curiosity and suspicion overthrowing the fluttering taking place in her stomach.

Her mother eyed the envelope, then smiled at Izzie brightly. "What do you suppose it says?"

Izzie met her mother's excited gaze. Whatever was inside, she didn't want to have to open it with an audience. She shrugged then folded the envelope in half and shoved it in her back pocket. "I don't know but it doesn't matter right now." She patted her mother's knee. "Because I'm here to visit with you. What do you say we read some of that book?"

Margaret nodded. "That's a wonderful idea."

Izzie flipped the envelope over in her hands. She'd held onto it for almost a full week and still hadn't been able to bring herself to investigate its contents. It didn't look like anything special. For all she knew, it could be a bill for that incredibly expensive book Bart had purchased. Heck, she wouldn't put it past Bart to use this as a way to manipulate her.

She tossed it frisbee style onto her bed and wandered over toward the window that gave her the perfect view of the casino. What she wouldn't give to have enough money to move somewhere else—away from the casino and everything it stood for.

Her eyes grazed the people coming and going. The later in the day it became, the heavier the flow of people who entered the building. She found herself searching for a specific someone then berated herself for it and let out a sharp, exasperated sigh before heading back toward her bedroom door.

At this point, Bart was a parasite taking up valuable space in her mind.

Maybe parasite was too strong of a word. He might not have the morals she did, but he'd already shown himself worthy of being given the benefit of the doubt. And seeing the happiness he'd brought her mother—she blew out another breath. At some point she'd have to stop trying so hard to push him away.

She turned and eyed the envelope on her bed then took

a step toward it when a buzzing sound filled the apartment. Izzie jumped and hurried over to the intercom by her front door. She held down the button, "Yes?"

"Izzie? It's Olivia."

"Liv? What are you doing here? Is Mom okay?"

Her staticky voice came through the system. "What? Of course she is. But it's the last Saturday of the month. Don't tell me you forgot."

Izzie sighed and leaned against the wall. "I don't really feel like doing karaoke tonight, Liv."

"Oh no you don't. We do this every month. If you don't buzz me up, I'll bribe someone to let me in anyway. I won't let you become a recluse, Izzie."

She rested her head against the wall. She should just ignore Olivia, but she knew better. Olivia would make good on her threat. There was no way she'd be able to avoid karaoke night. She turned around and jabbed her thumb against the button that unlocked the door to the front of the building.

It only took Olivia a few minutes to get up to Izzie's floor. She knocked three times before she just opened the door and let herself inside.

Olivia arrived in a flurry. She wore a bright smile to accentuate her bright clothes. The dress she wore was a flamboyant pink and went perfectly with a pair of matching flats. She had her black hair styled in beach waves and she didn't even take a breath before plopped herself onto Izzie's couch. "You're not wearing *that*, are you?"

Izzie stared down at her jeans and lightweight, long sleeved green t-shirt. She met Olivia's gaze and folded her arms tightly across her chest. "I told you, I don't feel like going out tonight."

Olivia heaved herself off of the couch and make a

tisking sound with her tongue. "When your mother got placed at Maple Gardens, what did you want to do then?" Izzie rolled her eyes and folded her arms. This was always the route Olivia took when she wanted to win an argument.

"You wanted to stay inside and let the world pass by you. But what did we do? We found a place that does karaoke night every month and you were able to move past the disappointment and the heartache." Olivia practically floated through the apartment toward Izzie's room. Her voice was more distant but still clear. "So you're going to get dressed and we are going to—" She reappeared in the doorway holding the envelope up with one hand. "What's this?"

Launching out of the chair, Izzie threw herself toward Olivia. "Give that to me."

Her friend held it just out of reach, preventing Izzie from being able to snatch it from her hand. Olivia's eyes narrowed then widened slowly as understanding dawned in her face. "No," she whispered. She stared at the envelope with fresh eyes. "Don't tell me Bart—"

Izzie seized the envelope and thrust it behind her back. "I don't know."

Olivia placed a hand on a propped hip and tilted her head. "Don't lie to me, Izzie. I always know when you're lying."

"Fine. He left this in that book he got my mom."

Olivia's wide-eyed stare did nothing to ease the tension in the room. She stared at the envelope again with an almost hungry expression. "Isobel Davis! You've had a letter from a billionaire for an entire week and you didn't open it?" She shook her head sharply. "Strike that. You've had a letter from a billionaire for a full week and you didn't tell *me* about it?" She placed a hand on her heart and pouted. "I'm hurt. Am I not your best friend who helps you make the worst decisions?" She reached for the letter but Izzie took a step back.

"I'm not sure I want to open it."

"Why not?" Olivia folded her arms, the frown on her face more prominent. "Bartholomew Brown is the most eligible bachelor either one of us will ever know. He's wealthy, nice, and don't forget—*hot*. It's obvious he likes you. There's not one single reason why you shouldn't go after him." She finally got her hands on the envelope and studied it. "He's got nice handwriting too. You know what they say about that."

"He's not my type, Liv. Just drop it." Izzie shoved past her friend, grabbing the letter, and moved into her room. "I'll go to that stupid karaoke night, okay? Let's just not talk about him anymore." She opened the drawer in her bedside table and tossed the letter inside. When she turned around, Olivia was standing in the doorway, her shoulder leaning against the door jamb. It was unnerving the way she could stare at Izzie like she knew exactly what was going on in her head.

Izzie shifted, squirming under that scrutiny. Forcing herself to adjust the train of thinking she'd been riding, she wrung her hands together. "Is there any way we can just stay in tonight? I don't even have my guitar anymore." There were several reasons she didn't want to do karaoke this month in particular. Paying for her mother's care had been just a little too much. It would be the first month she'd have to sing without it. On top of that, she'd hit dead end after dead end while searching for her mother's jade necklace.

On top of those issues, now there was a billionaire— who as much as she wanted to—she couldn't hate him. His morals didn't align with hers but the way he treated his uncle and her mother made it so hard to brush him off.

"Izzie, are you listening to me?"

She jumped. "What?"

Her friend gave her a pointed look and Izzie blushed. Olivia moved into the room and laid her hands on Izzie's shoulders. "We've been over this. Sometimes you have to do something that you don't want to do because it will help you—strengthen you. If I let those residents at Maple Gardens avoid things they weren't in the mood for, I'd have several unhappy people to take care of." She tilted her head. "Humor me? Let's go out and get your mind off of everything that is bothering you."

It wasn't any use. By the time she got back, everything would come crashing back as reality settled on her shoulders.

The only problem at this point in time was how Olivia would feel if Izzie backed out of her promise. She forced a smile and nodded. "Yeah. Okay. Let me get ready and we can get going."

Chapter Eight

Bart paced his office at the casino, running his hand through his already mussed hair. The casino was making money. His uncle was being well-cared for. Everything he'd been selling off has been prepared for donating to charity. So why did he feel so off balance?

He shot a look at the calendar that was open on his computer screen. One week. It had been one week since he'd given Margaret the book. Was it possible that she hadn't found the letter he'd tucked inside?

Bart dragged a hand down his face. He should have just given Izzie the envelope before he left. Now, he didn't know if she'd even gotten it so he couldn't exactly go track her down and ask her about it.

It wasn't anything special. At the time when he'd written it, he'd thought himself clever. He'd given her his number so the ball could be in her court. He would have figured that she'd have opened it, and contacted him if only to tell him that she was flattered but not interested.

By that point, he'd have *her* number and he could turn into that squeaky wheel.

Bart groaned inwardly. Now he was really sounding desperate. If Izzie didn't want to see him, he should take the hint and leave her alone. The problem with that was —*everything*.

She was there in his dreams while he slept. She was in his thoughts as he visited with his uncle. And he couldn't help but look up at her apartment building every dang time he went in to work. Izzie's face plagued his thoughts worse than any addiction man had to deal with over the centuries.

He stopped his pacing and placed both palms on his desk. He'd come in here to think about how to improve the entertainment aspect of the casino. The building could be used for so much more. There was a potential that hadn't been tapped yet, he just needed to find it. The more money he made, the more potential for the charitable works he could participate in.

A soft knock on the door drew his head up. His latest assistant poked her head inside. "I'm terribly sorry, sir, but the magic act that was supposed to perform next weekend has had to cancel."

"That's the third time this month," he muttered.

"Would you like me to find someone to fill in their slot?" She didn't move from her location, her eyes glued to his.

Bart waved her off. "No. I'll figure out something." Just as she was about to retreat, he bounded around the desk. "Why do we only do shows on the weekend?"

"Sir?"

"Why do we only book shows for the weekend? Why not every night of the week?"

She blinked at him and he sliced his hand through the air again, turning to head back to his desk.

"We should be utilizing that space every single night." He turned to face her, "I'm sorry, what was your name?"

"Trina."

"Trina. Right. Well, Trina, we need to start booking other events, not just the big ones, but the small ones, too." He snapped his fingers a few times. "There's a coffee shop down the street that does karaoke on Saturday nights—"

"Just the last Saturday, sir."

"What?" He peered at her.

Trina swallowed and placed her hands behind her back, her eyes darting away from him. She cleared her throat and finally swung her focus back to him. "They only do karaoke on the last Saturday of the month—but it's always packed."

"Do you think we could get people in here to do a bigger event? What if we did a karaoke competition where the winner gets a big prize?"

Her features brightened. "I think that's a great idea."

He moved around his desk and rifled through the papers on it. "That's one idea. I need you to get me at least six more."

"Sir?"

Bart glanced up at her and offered a patient smile. "We need to get people out here every night of the week—not necessarily for the casino side of things—for the entertainment, too. I want this place to be the hang-out people didn't realize has been missing from their lives."

She nodded. "Yes, sir."

"Oh! Trina?"

She poked her head back inside the door. "Yes?"

"Get me the address for that place that does the karaoke nights. I want to see what kind of interest we have here."

Trina nodded once more and disappeared. Bart might not have gone to business school. Heck, he might not have been born for this job. But he had to admit he'd fallen into the role better than anyone could have expected.

At least the company was still up and running.

He reached for his suit coat that hung on a hook near the window behind his desk and slipped his arms inside. The best way to get to know a new business was by observation. By the time he headed out into the reception area, Trina had the address scrawled across a small piece of paper. He offered her a small smile. "I should only be a few hours. If I don't get back by eight, lock up for me, will you?"

"Yes, sir."

One elevator ride, one taxicab drive, and several minutes in traffic later, he found himself standing in front of a coffee shop that almost looked exactly like the one in that romantic comedy tv series that ran for ten years.

Bart tipped his cab driver generously and exited the vehicle. He strode straight for the front door and stepped inside. The place was packed. Only standing room for anyone who'd made the mistake of coming late. Every chair, stool, and sofa chair had been claimed. A handful of people hovered near the front where they'd be able to make their song request.

This place was more packed than anywhere he'd ever been, even for a Saturday night. If he were to follow the trend, he could offer the casino's theatre room to groups of people like this to either raise money or bring in more customers. And after Trina came up with several more ideas, the casino would become something his uncle could have only dreamed of it becoming.

He ducked through the groups of people until he found a space toward the back where he wasn't forced to be squished between someone who used too much perfume and another who made the same mistake with body spray. If he was lucky, he might find some fresh talent for the casino.

The thought *had* crossed his mind to ask Izzie if she would have been interested, but she'd refused to show him any indication she could hold a tune. Just because she could play guitar didn't mean she could sing.

A waitress slipped through the crowd and if she'd been any more graceful, she'd have to have been a ballerina. She carried a tray of glasses filled nearly to the brim with varying liquids but managed not to spill a single drop. It was fascinating to be sure and far more entertaining than waiting for the next singer to get on stage.

That was, until a familiar flash of auburn hair caught his eye. Immediately, Bart's focus returned to the stage as non-other than Isobel Davis got seated. She accepted a microphone from the MC and smiled as the crowd let out a cheer.

Bart chuckled as he glanced around the room. Apparently she was some kind of regular. The beginning notes to a song by Rascal Flatts started. Chills swept through his body as she closed her eyes and swayed to the words she sang. It was like she was singing about someone specific. There was no way this song didn't mean something to her.

Her voice hit a crescendo so perfectly he couldn't drag his eyes from her. So much pain and yearning and all he wanted to do was climb onto that stage and pull her into his arms. His heart ached for her.

The problem was that he could never do that. If she even knew he was here, he'd get another one of her lectures about stalking her. And this time he really hadn't tried to find her. It was like the universe wanted them to cross paths.

It was a dangerous game to be sure. Fighting fate could hold dangerous consequences. Izzie finished her song and the entire coffee shop erupted with screams and applause.

She looked out over the crowd, a wide smile on her face until her eyes landed on him. Suddenly that smile disappeared.

Another chill swept through him but this time it was for a different reason. Uh oh. She'd spotted him. He glanced around, seeking out the closest exit. Normally, he'd just confront her and tell her just how amazing her voice was. Girls got a kick out of those kinds of complements. But for whatever reason, Izzie wasn't one of those girls.

He'd only managed to get a water, but he hated not leaving a tip, so he slapped a five-dollar bill on the table and jumped from the stool where he sat. Had the crowd grown bigger? There was no way for him to get to the exit in a timely manner and already, he could see she'd set her sights on him. He needed to get out of there.

Bart backed up, spinning around but not seeing that the ballerina waitress was right behind him. He bumped into her, reaching out to hopefully steady not only himself but her and managed only to grab onto the large circular tray she balanced on the palm of her hand.

The tray tipped toward him.

As if in slow motion the whole thing flipped over. Large plastic glasses containing sodas, smaller shot glasses with amber liquid, and a couple cups of water all came crashing down around the two of them.

Those who were paying attention jumped back and out of the way. The less fortunate ones let out gasps of surprise as they were hit by the backsplash of every drop landing on him and at his feet. His white dress shirt was now completely doused and sticking to his torso.

Bart shook out his arms, flinging droplets in all directions and garnering scowls from those in his crosshairs.

He felt her gaze on him before turning to find Izzie

standing mere inches away. Her scowl matched those around her but for different reasons. Her arms were folded across her chest and she shook her head in exasperation. "Why do you keep following me?"

Bart held up a finger. "I think the real question ought to be, why do we keep meeting like this?"

Her mouth quirked into a half-smile. "Honestly, I don't think I'd mind you stalking me so much if this was the outcome each time."

"Izzie, be nice!" A familiar face materialized out of the crowd. Olivia. She stepped forward with a handful of napkins. "You poor thing."

"Serves him right for fleeing the scene of the crime," Izzie smirked but quickly hid it when her friend gave her a dirty look.

"For that, you should offer to take him to your place to clean up."

Izzie's brows shot up. "What? Absolutely *not*."

Olivia placed her hands on her hips. "Izzie. He's cold and wet and you probably live closer than anyone else."

"I can just go back to the casino. It's no problem."

Izzie gestured toward him. "See? He's fine."

Her friend faced him. "Is there a washer at your casino?"

"Well, no, but—"

"See, Izzie? That shirt looks expensive—"

"Actually it's—"

"—And he needs a fresh shirt." Her friend beamed. "It's the least you could do after he gave your mom that book."

Izzie gaped at her friend then her gaze shot to Bart. "Fine. But I don't think I have anything that will fit him."

Her friend rolled her eyes and faced him. "Don't let her

fool you. She's got plenty of band t-shirts from the days when she was practically a roadie."

Bart looked toward Izzie again. "Really? I didn't think you—"

"Not a word," she muttered. "Come on. Let's go." She made it a few steps with him following close behind her when she suddenly realized her friend wasn't with her. Izzie stopped suddenly and turned around, causing him to nearly bump into a second woman in one night. She stood on her toes and called out, "Liv, you coming?"

Her friend waved toward her and shook her head. "Nah. I think I'll stay. See you later."

"But—"

"Later, Izzie!" Her friend winked before turning back to a young man she was speaking to.

Izzie dragged her attention back to him and frowned. "Come on," she sighed. "I'll put your shirt in the wash but I'm not drying it."

Chapter Nine

Izzie fought the urge to stomp up every flight of stairs to her apartment. How had she managed to get roped into helping the one guy she didn't want to see? Either the universe had a very strange sense of humor or she was cursed.

"I didn't know you could sing."

She stiffened. Bart's voice sounded so close despite him being a few steps away from her. It was like he was whispering in her ear. "I'm not very good."

"I beg to differ." He was closing in on her and the hairs on the back of her neck stood on end. "You could be on that reality television show where they find music stars."

Izzie snorted. "That show is for professionals. There's no way I could be in their league."

He laughed, sending a wave of goosebumps along her arms. "When was the last time you watched that show? I'm serious. You have some really good pipes. You should audition for something like that."

"I don't have time." Her statement was true, but there were also deeper reasons for not even allowing herself to dream about performing in front of a real crowd. One was the fact it might take her away from her mother. But mostly it was because music didn't hold the same joy it used to. Ever since she'd had to sell her guitar, she hadn't felt connected to the music.

Every so often a performance like tonight would get to her. Apparently it had gotten to him, too. Speaking of which. She spun around right as they made it to her apartment door. "So spill. Did you put a tracker on my phone or something?"

He laughed again. "What?"

"My phone. That's how you keep finding me, right?"

To his credit, the confusion on Bart's face looked so authentic he could have been an actor. Maybe he was one. How else could he break past her defenses and make it so hard to dislike him? Bart shoved his hands in his pockets. "You want the truth?"

She sighed. "Obviously."

"I'm trying to come up with some more show ideas for the casino."

The casino. Of course he was. Guys like Bartholomew Brown only cared about making money. She rolled her eyes and turned to open her door.

His hand shot out and grasped hers. There was a strange sort of smile on his face and he tilted his head. "What was that?"

"What was *what*?"

"That look you gave me."

She shook her head, warmth spreading like spilled milk across her cheeks. "I didn't give you a look."

"You rolled your eyes."

"No, I didn't." Did she? If she did it must have become second nature while she was around him. She needed to be more careful.

"Yes, you did. Why did you do that?"

Izzie threw up her hands, yanking the one he held from his grasp. "I don't know. I do that sometimes when I think that someone is being ridiculous."

He chuckled again. Boy, she wished he'd stop doing that. At the rate things were going, her goosebumps were going to be permanent. "You think me keeping my uncle's business afloat is ridiculous?"

"I think owning and operating a casino is ridiculous." She shoved her key into the doorknob and unlocked it. Without waiting to hear his response, she hurried inside. The more distance she could put between them, the better. It was already getting hard to keep her attention from slipping lower to see his chiseled chest beneath his wet shirt.

Izzie tossed her keys into a dish on the coffee table in the living room then shrugged out of her jacket. She took out her phone, noticing that Olivia had already messaged her. Well, too bad. She wasn't going to update her friend until she saw her at Maple Gardens. Served her right for meddling.

Bart stood just inside the closed door, his gaze sweeping through her apartment and probably judging her for how small it was. The apartment was a one-bedroom with barely enough room for a love seat and a table for two. He could probably fit the entire thing in his living room.

She pointed down the hall. "The bathroom is on the right. I'll grab you one of my t-shirts and you can change in there." She headed toward her room, grateful for the opportunity to get some added distance. She could probably wash his shirt in about twenty minutes if she put it on a quick cycle. Then he'd be out of there.

She found an old worn-out t-shirt with an ABBA logo on it and wandered back into the living room. A gasp tore from her throat and she spun around. Bart had already removed his shirt and he stood near her apartment window staring down at the casino—*his* casino.

His back faced her, but it was just as toned as his front —at least from what she could tell beneath his saturated shirt.

He must have heard her entrance because he let out that infuriating chuckle again.

Izzie held out the shirt and shook it in his general direction but refused to look at him. "Here. Put this on." She heard him approach then stop. He didn't take the shirt from her right away. Instead, he teased her.

"You're not embarrassed to see a shirtless man, are you? Am I correct in assuming you've never been to the beach?"

"Of course I have," she snapped. "But we're not at the beach, are we?" She shook the shirt again. "Just get dressed. Please." Her face was already burning and the scarlet coloring would likely not fade before he left, thanks to her red hair.

Bart grabbed the shirt, and his fingers grazed hers.

Jolts of electricity flickered and sparked from their touch. She jumped and dropped the shirt. The fabric landed with a light thump on the ground but Bart swiped it before she could. She turned a little too early, the shirt was over his head, but didn't cover his chest.

Her mouth went dry and she looked away again. The wet shirt he'd worn hadn't hidden much of anything. The guy must have a strict workout regimen to look so good.

Stop it! You're not some hormonal teenager gawking at your crush. He's just a man.

An infuriatingly generous man whose laugh could make her skin react as if she'd just stepped inside a deep freezer after being in the summer heat. It might be refreshing, but it was chilling at the same time.

She darted around him, retrieving the shirt he'd left in a crumpled heap on her coffee table. Before he could say a word, she slipped past him again, brushing against his arm and headed toward the laundry room. It took all of five minutes to throw the shirt in the wash with a soap pod and return to the living room. This time she was careful to keep her eyes trained on the floor.

When she brought her gaze back to his, she found him smiling at her, his head tilted in a way that a predator might when examining this prey. Izzie shifted and scooted a few feet away from him.

Thankfully, he moved back to the window. "So this is what you meant when you said you could see me."

Her blush deepened when he glanced back at her.

Bart turned around and leaned against the windowsill. "I know you've mentioned a few reasons why you dislike me and most of it has to do with the casino. Care to elaborate?"

She scowled at him, finding a seat and plopping down on the overstuffed chair. "No thank you."

He moved through the room, examining the books on her shelves, framed pictures on her wall, and coming to stop at a hook just beneath them. "What's this?"

Her gaze dipped to the hook and bounced back to his face. "That is—was—for my guitar."

"*Was*?" His brows pinched then understanding dawned on his beautiful features. "You said you played."

"I *did*."

"Well, where is it?"

"What don't you get about the word 'was'? I don't have a guitar anymore."

He touched the hook almost reverently. "Why not?"

She blew out a frustrated breath. "I'm not going to tell you my life story, Bart. Frankly, I feel like you know a little too much already. It's unnerving how many questions you keep asking me."

He settled into a seat of his own and leaned forward, his elbows resting on his knees. "Okay, just one more question. Did you open that letter I left with your mother?"

She stiffened and the blush that had miraculously dissipated returned with a vengeance. She looked away and muttered. "No." There was no use lying about even receiving the thing. He was quiet for far too long, so she looked over at him. "What?"

Bart sat up and lifted a shoulder. "Nothing."

"No, that wasn't nothing. You're judging me, aren't you?"

"Isn't that what you've been doing to me since the moment we met?"

She heaved a heavy breath and shifted in her seat. "I make judgements based on real-life experiences. And those experiences tell me everything I need to know about you."

He scratched his cheek and tilted his head again. The lump in her throat grew and she couldn't swallow it down even if she wanted to. She absolutely hated the way he was looking at her like he could read her thoughts.

Izzie folded her arms tightly across her chest and frowned at him. "Will you *stop* that?"

"Stop what, exactly?" He laughed again. "Looking at you? Would you prefer I wander through your home again and ask you a million questions?"

She groaned. The next twenty minutes were going to be the longest ones of her life.

"Would it really be so hard to tell me why you despise me so much?"

She threw her head back and looked at the patterns on the ceiling. Why was she so against telling him? It wasn't like she was ashamed of her opinions. Shame only reared its ugly head when she had to talk about her father.

"Fine," she muttered. "Tell me, what is the purpose of a casino? The most basic one."

His features pinched and he gave her a crooked smile. "Is this a trick question?"

She shook her head and leaned forward. "No. I'm making a point."

He settled into his chair a little more. "It's a place for people to blow off steam. They get to come and take a break from their lives and have a little fun."

"Wrong."

Bart studied her for a moment. "I'm sorry, who is the one who owns the casino?"

She let out an exaggerated sigh, ignoring his question. "Casinos exist for one reason. They are a place that steals money from people who think they have a chance at walking out of that building," she jabbed a finger toward the window, "with a jackpot. Those poor people come into your establishment, gamble away their paychecks and leave with nothing."

His eyes narrowed. "Are you suggesting that I'm the one to blame when that happens? I hate to break it to you. But those people are mature adults who can make their own choices."

Izzie snorted and looked away. "And what about the drunks or those who have an addiction? Do you do anything to help them when they obviously should be anywhere but in your place of business?"

He didn't speak for several moments, spurring her to look in his direction just once more. Understanding dawned in his gaze. "Did that happen to someone you know?"

She shot out of her seat and strode toward the kitchen. "I'm thirsty. You want a drink?" Izzie didn't wait for a response. She grabbed two plastic cups from the cupboard and took them to the refrigerator to fill them with ice. Bart had no right to dig into her personal life and pass judgment. She was entitled to her opinions of the people who came and went from the building just outside her window. If that bothered Bartholomew Brown, he could just quit his job and do something more meaningful with his life.

Chapter Ten

The pieces were finally coming together. Little by little he was beginning to understand what made Izzie tick. Of course the first woman who had caught his eye had a bad experience with a casino. Those kinds of stories weren't that rare, but the people who held onto them were.

It was just his luck that Izzie was one of them.

He shifted in his seat and gazed at her as she filled the cups with water. The whole thing made her uncomfortable, so the experience would have been closer to home. A sibling perhaps? A parent? He knew her mother and Margaret didn't seem like the type. Her father?

Izzie practically shoved the glass into his hands before she moved back to her seat. She sipped her drink and refused to meet his gaze. There was a fresh layer of color on her cheeks that gave her more of a glow than anything else.

The air hung thick with a tension that hadn't been there before. How was he supposed to explain to her that he wasn't anything at all like she described? Even if he could come up with the words, they'd likely sound trite or like he was making excuses.

He swirled the liquid in his cup around and around, watching the ice knock into each other before he lifted his focus to Izzie. "You know, not all casinos are out to make money."

She snorted.

"I mean it." He leaned forward and placed his cup on the coffee table. "I inherited that casino."

Izzie huffed. "Just because you inherited it doesn't mean that you don't have a board you're required to keep happy."

"True. *However*, the board who oversees all the businesses I inherited give me some leeway when it comes to certain holdings." He watched her, praying that she'd be intrigued enough to relax a little.

Her gaze flicked to him. He bit back his smile upon seeing the curiosity he read there. "Did you know that my uncle owned eight casinos in the surrounding states?"

Izzie's eyes rounded but she didn't comment.

"Yep. And I sold all of them except one." He pointed at the window. "That one was his first so I kept it for sentimental reasons." He shrugged again, then looked down at his hands. "Most of the money I made on the sales were donated to charity, because he also left me with more money than I know what to do with." When he glanced at her again, the hardness of her eyes seemed to have disappeared completely. "You didn't read about any of that in the tabloids, did you?"

"No," she murmured.

"Yeah. Those guys tend to be more interested in gossip than the philanthropic decisions I make. So while you make a good point regarding casinos, they aren't all bad. Or, rather the owners aren't all bad." This statement earned him a small smile.

"I'd be naïve to believe anything you just said at face value." She brought her drink to her lips and took a sip. "I will most definitely be factchecking all of it."

Bart chuckled. "I'd be disappointed if you did anything less."

She placed her cup on the coffee table then pulled her legs up beneath her. She looked away again, her expression sobering. "If everything you said is true, I hope you know that you're an anomaly."

"How so?" This woman was something else. At every turn she had some new comment that should probably annoy him, but it only endeared her to him more.

Izzie's lips twitched and she shook her head. "What kind of guy buys a collectible first edition book just because some stranger says they like it? On that same note, only a crazy person would just willingly give it away."

He cocked his head to the side. There it was again. She was struggling financially. His gaze swept through the room to the guitar hook and the missing instrument. She must be supporting her mother all on her own. The apartment they sat in was a closet compared to what Uncle Larry had left him—not that he wanted it. He fully intended on selling the property, but hadn't gotten around to it.

Bart stared at Izzie with fresh understanding. Money was important to her—something she didn't have. Even before he'd inherited everything from Larry, he had never come against a deadline to pay a bill and worried where the money would come from. It wouldn't surprise him in the least if Izzie dealt with that on a regular basis.

"Hello? Are you even listening?"

He jumped and found Izzie staring at him with mild concern.

"You okay?"

Nodding, he reached for his glass and took a sip. "Peachy."

"Anyway. On top of everything else, it's not normal for a human being to go from average to wealthy and not completely make a mess of things. I mean, look at the last lottery winner. Most of those folks blow through millions in only a couple years."

He held up a finger. "To be fair, most millionaires are only worth what they own in stocks. From what I understand, several of them don't have the liquid assets you're referring to."

Her face scrunched up and she mimicked him. "*From what I understand...*" she laughed. "Do you hear yourself? You *are* one of those people, Bart. You are worth millions."

Billions actually. But she didn't need to know that. "I do have a large bank account. But most of my wealth is in the properties I own. My uncle invested wisely in that respect." His brows furrowed once more. "Isn't it unseemly to discuss finances? I'd much rather talk about your singing talents."

And just like that Izzie shut him out. Her face went blank and she twisted in her seat to stare at the wall. "There isn't much to say."

"I beg to differ. Based on what you sang tonight—"

"Just drop it, Bart. I'm not interested in talking about that sort of stuff."

Point taken. Maybe he'd get her to warm up to him another time. The washer dinged, signaling the shirt was done. Izzie jumped from her seat and hurried out of the room. She returned with a bag and held it out to him. "There. All washed. You can hang it to dry or tell your maid to put it in the dryer for you."

He didn't accept her offering right away. "You have a very poor understanding of what my life is like."

"This again? Dude, all I need to know I already do. Between the news outlets, the tabloids, and watching you come and go, I think I've pretty much got it covered."

"Except you haven't." He stood from his seat, straightening to his full height. Her chin lifted as her gaze remained locked on his. He got a small amount of pleasure from the way she took a small step back. "You have this outdated view of me because you refuse to see me as a person."

Her head reared back and her eyes narrowed. "I see you as a person."

Bart shook his head. "I beg to differ. All you see are dollar signs."

She gasped. "I'm not after your money."

"I wouldn't dream of suggesting that. *No*, you see dollar signs and rather than ask for me to give you money, you pass judgment on me. Both prevent you from getting to know the real me."

Izzie shoved the bag at him once more. "I don't need to get to know the real you. So just take your shirt and don't forget to shut the door all the way when you leave."

Bart tisked and shook his head. "I'll leave, but first you have to promise me one thing."

She let out a groan. "You realize this is my home and if I ask you to go but you refuse, you're officially trespassing. I could call the police."

One brow arched and he gave her a half-smile. "I don't believe you would stoop to such levels. Especially not when agreeing to one simple thing would get me out of your hair far more quickly." He was wearing her down. He could see it in the way she shifted and her frame relaxed.

He could practically observe the cogs in her mind whirring and spinning as she weighed the risks involved.

"Fine. What exactly do you want me to agree to?"

Bart leaned forward, his face dipping closer. "I want you to go on a date with me."

She shot him a wide-eyed stare. "What? Absolutely not."

Well, that wasn't the response he'd been expecting. Since he'd inherited everything from his uncle, finding dates hadn't been hard at all. Most of the time the women he passed on the streets or met at clubs threw themselves at him. But then, Izzie wasn't like most women. She was different in a way that he found utterly intriguing. It might be the fact that she pushed him away at every turn.

But there was no denying how his body had reacted the first time he'd laid eyes on her. It was just disappointing that she passed such harsh judgments against him due to something that was out of his control.

He ran a hand through his now mussed hair. The silence between them grew as he considered the best course of action. Of which he could only think of just one. He could beg.

"What do you want me to do?"

Confusion flooded her features. It was likely due to the amount of time that had passed between them without words spoken. She took another small step backward, but the back of her legs bumped against the coffee table and she had nowhere else she could escape to. "What do you mean?"

"Should I grovel? I could drop to my knees right here and now and beg you to go on a date with me."

He didn't think it was possible but her eyes rounded even larger than before. "You wouldn't."

Bart snickered. "Like I said, you don't know me very well. You seem to have forgotten I was a normal guy before I inherited everything my uncle gave me. That means I was raised similarly to you. Sure, I could promise to fly you out on a private jet to parts unknown or to a private island—"

"You have a private island?" She blurted.

He cocked his head to the side and the corners of his mouth quirked into a small smile. "Would you say yes if I admitted to it?"

Her face colored again. "No."

"Then it doesn't matter what private island off the coast of New Zealand I may or may not own. What matters is that I won't take you anywhere you wouldn't be comfortable going. So I guess that limits us to the convenience store, Maple Gardens, that coffee place where I had my shirt ruined, and maybe a Taco Bell."

She snorted, then her hand clapped over her mouth and she dropped her gaze to the floor.

Bart hooked his finger under her chin, forcing her to look at him. She blinked her large jade-green eyes at him, her long lashes fluttering against her cheeks. His chest tightened. She had to be the most beautiful girl he'd ever met and the strangest part was she didn't even realize it. Lowering his voice to a husky whisper, he murmured, "Nothing would make me happier than if you went out on a date with me, Izzie."

Chapter Eleven

Chills, hot and cold raced through her body lifting small goosebumps like waves in an ocean. Izzie's mouth went dry and her heart thundered. Bart had just crossed a line. Not the bad kind—she wasn't upset. No, that wasn't it.

This line was something she never thought existed. He was quickly making her second guess everything she thought about him—everything she knew about him. His finger was warm where he held her chin captive. His brown eyes reminded her of smooth, melted chocolate.

There was something about him that made her want to lean in toward him and simply accept his request. Funnily enough, it was more than his looks and his money. She wasn't drawn to that. If anything, it was the book he'd gotten her mother. It was how he appeared so down to earth.

Would it be so bad to agree to *one* date? It couldn't hurt anything. He was just a guy—a guy with money and a casino and...

She pulled her chin from his grasp, her eyes narrowing. "I don't understand why you're being so persistent. I'm nothing special. Is this some weird 'you want what you can't have' sort of thing? Because—"

Bart laughed, cutting her off.

She studied him warily.

"Contrary to popular belief, not all men chase what they can't have. Think about it, Izzie. If a guy is only interested in the chase, when will enough be enough? Eventually he gets what he's chasing. Then where does that put him. Some guys just want to take out a pretty and talented woman because she stirs things within him that he wants to explore further."

Her mouth dropped open. Did he actually say that?

Bart stepped toward her again, his smile fading. "Look. I'm not in the business of chasing. You've already made this harder than it needed to be and I stuck around. If you earnestly don't want to go on a date with me," he held up placating hands, "then I won't force you. But let me say just this one last thing." He paused as if doing so would make her consider his words for what they were and not who they were coming from. "When was the last time you took a chance on something new, only to find out that you were missing out on something great? Sure, you could turn me down. You could rationalize that I'm not worth your time. You could even admit to yourself you're a little scared. But I don't think you will."

"You don't?" she whispered.

He shook his head. His hand came up and tucked a strand of hair out of her face and behind her ear. His warm touch sent shivers down her spin as he trailed his fingertips along her jaw where he grasped her chin once more. He leaned close and she sucked in sharply but didn't pull away.

Bart's warm breath tickled her skin. "No, I don't.

Because deep down you can sense that you feel something. You can't explain it but then maybe you don't want to."

Her lungs burned from holding her breath, waiting, expecting for him to steal a kiss. Then he stepped back and the cool air around them whooshed between them. She exhaled slowly, her heart pattering skittishly behind her ribs. When she brought her gaze up to meet his, she nearly expected to find a smug smile on his face.

Instead, all she found was a steady gaze full of question. He wanted her to answer him. Bartholomew Brown could have easily stolen a kiss from her lips but instead he'd remained a gentleman.

Izzie pulled her lower lip between her teeth, hating the way her lips seemed to tingle in anticipation of being kissed by the tall, dark, handsome millionaire who currently wore one of her old t-shirts. "Okay. Fine," she stammered. "*One* date."

His face broke into a wide smile—a smile that only exacerbated the flutters and churning that currently took place in her chest. "That's all I'll need." He grabbed the plastic bag containing his damp shirt, tossed it in the air and caught it with the same hand. Then he spun on his heel and headed for the door, leaving her stunned.

"All you need for what? Wait, are you going?"

Bart held up a hand, not turning to face her, and waved. "As I said, the second you agreed to my terms I was willing to leave in a moment's notice."

She hurried toward him. "So that's it then. You're just going to leave and then we're going on a date and then what? What did you mean, 'that's all you'll need'?"

He stopped as he reached the door, frozen, causing her to have to stop suddenly or bump into him. Bart glanced over his shoulder and flashed her a smile that quickly disappeared. Those dark eyes of his seemed to break through the walls she had carefully constructed and all she could focus on was that he knew every single thought racing through her head at that moment.

Maybe she didn't want him to leave just yet. Maybe she was starting to warm up to him. Maybe she was actually going crazy. She shouldn't have chased him to the door to stop him from leaving.

Izzie shifted her weight from one foot to the other and shoved her hands in her pockets. Her face filled with heat and she looked away. When he took a step closer, her eyes darted up to meet his.

"Am I correct in assuming you're warming up to me?"

She fought the instinct to throw some off-colored comment toward him. Instead she shrugged. "If I were you, I wouldn't be so bold as to assume anything in this situation. Perhaps you just wore me down and I did what I had to in order to get you out of my apartment."

"That's fair." His gaze swept over her. She'd never felt so vulnerable in her entire life. "Let me put it this way. The only assumption about me that you got right is that I'm confident."

"I never said—" Noting the way his eyes seemed to dance with humor, she cut herself off. He was teasing her.

Bart continued. "In most situations, I exude confidence. But I'll let you in on a little secret. It's not because I have money or because my social standing demands it. I learned my confidence on the battlefield. Those teenagers can be vicious when they get a substitute teacher."

Izzie gaped. But before she could ask him to elaborate, he offered her a wave and ducked out into the hallway. By the time she'd managed to open her door and head out there after him, he'd already turned a corner.

Still in a stunned state, she returned to her apartment and shut the door as she leaned against it. Bart was a teacher? Well, not anymore, obviously. She could have imagined him in almost any career. But a *teacher*? She wouldn't have thought of that in a million years.

Something akin to shame washed over her. Bart had been nothing but nice to her—a little pushy, maybe—but nice. And her excuse for judging him was the fact that he owned his uncle's casino.

The intensity of the heat in her face increased. Izzie covered her face with her hands and groaned. How embarrassing. There was still a slim chance he wasn't what he appeared to be. For all she knew, he could be lying. But why lie about something so mundane.

"A teacher?" Izzie marched over to the window and stared down at the street. Bart crossed the street in his suit pants, still wearing that ridiculous t-shirt. He got to the other side and stilled. Then his head tilted until she could see his face.

She jumped back, out of his view. It wasn't likely that he could tell her window from any of the others, but she'd rather not risk it. Peeking at him from behind her drapes, Izzie smiled along with him. He shook his head and strode into the casino, disappearing from sight.

About five minutes later, her phone buzzed on the coffee table. She headed across the room and picked it up. A message from Bart appeared on her screen.

I hope you don't mind. I put my number in your phone.
You can disregard the letter.

· · ·

She gnawed on her lower lip as her smile widened. He was persistent, she had to give him that. Of course he wouldn't leave without ensuring that he'd be able to get ahold of her. She could appreciate that sort of personality trait.

Her thumb hovered over the keyboard on her phone. She could message him. Or she could make him wait. Then again, hadn't she made him wait far too long already?

Izzie typed in a quick reply then tossed her phone on the couch.

Seems to me, you don't care whether I would mind or not.

Her phone lit up and buzzed again. She snatched the phone and brought up his three-word message.

You got me.

He was ridiculous. Surprisingly sweet but still ridiculous. Izzie put her phone back on the couch, finding she was actually looking forward to a date with Bartholomew Brown.

The flutters in Izzie's chest hadn't abated since that night when Bart had asked her out. Each time she stopped by Maple Gardens to visit her mother, the anticipation of seeing him increased ten-fold. He'd sent her a few more text messages but beyond that, he'd been rather absent.

The anticipation of seeing him continued to grow out of control. Then at the beginning of this week, he'd called her. The sound of his voice was enough to set her off balance and now as she was getting ready for their official date, she couldn't keep her hands from shaking.

Any woman in the world would have sacrificed their left foot to go on a date with a millionaire—especially with one as good-looking as Bart. He hadn't told her where they were going or what he had in mind which only made her more anxious. She didn't even know what she should wear. He'd said dress nice, but that could mean anything to a guy like him.

Izzie groaned and dragged her hands down her face as she stared at her reflection in the mirror. The sundress she'd picked swirled around her knees when she walked. It was cotton, but it appeared to be more formal than the average sundress. The dark green color matched her eyes, which was the only reason she picked it out.

She frowned as she grabbed a handful of the fabric in her fist. She should change into something more—more what?

Bart had seemed to have stepped back and given her space but that didn't mean he couldn't at least tell her what they were doing.

The doorbell buzzed. Too late to change now. Izzie took in a deep breath and then strode for the door. It was one date. Bart wasn't going to ask her to marry him or anything. She could do this. With her left hand, she yanked open the door.

He didn't face her. He wore a white shirt with sleeves rolled up to his elbows. His khaki pants were exactly as he'd suggested—nice—but not overdoing it. He turned and his gaze trailed over her outfit then found eyes. "Wow," he murmured. "You look—"

"You don't look half bad yourself." She tucked a strand of auburn hair behind her ear before clasping her hands together in front of her. "Are you going to finally tell me where we're going today?"

"*That*, is still a surprise." He gave her a crooked grin and held out his hand.

Izzie tilted her head, examining him with new eyes. She could see him, dressed like this in front of a classroom.

Bart looked away for just a second and chuckled. "What?"

She shrugged. "Nothing." Placing her hand in his, she allowed him to lead her down the stairs and out to the street to a waiting limousine. Izzie gave him a pointed look. "You can't be serious."

He waved off the footman and opened the door for her. "Everyone should be able to ride in one of these at least once in their life." Bart gestured for her to enter. "Besides. Where we're going, you're going to want to be comfortable."

Chapter Twelve

Once he'd gotten her to agree to a date, it had taken him two weeks to figure out the perfect place to take her. Bart's knees bounced as he watched Izzie stare out the limo window and he rested his hands on them in an attempt to stop.

It wasn't any use. His nerves had gotten the better of him and there was nothing he could do. He'd built up this whole experience in his head and to Izzie that one wrong turn could make or break it.

She met his gaze and let out a soft laugh. "You okay?"

"What? Of course I'm okay."

"Really? What happened to that raiding confidence you were so proud of?" She laughed again when his face fell.

"Well, I'll have you know that you are more terrifying than any of those students I had to teach." He didn't mean to say it. The words had just slipped from his mouth without being able to stop them.

Great. This would be it. He'd messed up his only chance to prove to her he wasn't what she thought him to be.

She placed a hand on his knee and shot him a soft smile.

Warmth seeped into his skin from her touch and he stared at her hand until she spoke again. "How about you tell me what it's like to be a teacher."

All at once the tension in his shoulders drained. A wide smile filled his face. "I teach—*taught*—English." He shifted in his seat. "It's amazing what those kids can learn from a story that's decades old—centuries even." He chattered on about what books and plays they were reading before he'd had to quit and run his uncle's holdings. It wasn't until they pulled up in front of an extravagant building that looked like it was made out of glass that he realized she hadn't gotten any words in edge-wise. Dang it, he'd messed up again. "I'm sorry. No one wants to hear about that sort of stuff."

"I do."

He stilled, his eyes narrowing slightly. "You're not serious."

She laughed. "Why wouldn't I be?"

"Well, for starters, the women I've been on dates with—"

Izzie held up her hand. "I'm going to stop you right there." She shook her head, her soft smile sending all sorts of electrical currents through his veins. "The women you've dated before are probably shallow and were only interested in one thing."

"My body?"

"Yes." Her eyes widened and she coughed. "No." Her face flushed a deep crimson color. "*No*, they want your money and your connections."

He scoffed. "What connections? I could introduce them to the principal of that middle school where I taught. I think she's written a romance novel."

Izzie's snort turned into a full bout of laughter. "I didn't realize you were so funny."

Bart beamed at her. "I guess we're both learning a lot of interesting things about each other."

"I guess so," she murmured. Her focus shifted toward the building out his window. "So, are you going to tell me what this place is or what?" She leaned over him, probably to get a better view and he was enveloped in a cloud of her perfume. His stomach tightened as he breathed in deeply. The light from the window reflected off her face and when she sat down she gave him a smile. "It's a beautiful building. I don't think I've ever been here before."

He reached into his back pocket and pulled out the pamphlet then presented it to her with a flourish.

Izzie reached for the brochure and opened it up. Her brows creased as she flipped through it. "An auction?"

Bart nodded. "Turn to page ten."

The coated pages flipped before them until she landed on page ten. His heart beat a little faster. This had to be it. He'd found it. Izzie's gaze scanned the page then she looked up at him chagrined. "Am I supposed to see something on here?"

Uh oh. He leaned forward. "Oh. It's on the next page." He flipped the page and then poked the paper about halfway down.

"A jade necklace with inscription." Her voice was so soft he almost didn't hear her. She flicked her gaze up to meet his. "There's no picture."

He grinned. "What do you say we go in there and see if it's the one?"

Shock. It was written all over her face. She didn't move, just stared at him.

"You...okay?"

Izzie blinked. The without provocation, she threw her arms around his neck. "I can't believe it," she murmured. "I can't believe you found it."

Slowly, he slipped his arms around her slight form. "Well, we're not sure if it's the *one*. But I think our chances are good."

She pulled back, brushed a tear from her cheek and gave him a short nod. "I think so, too."

The door beside him opened and Bart stepped out. He ducked down and held out his hand for Izzie to take. It was hard not to marvel at just how perfectly her hand looked within his own. But when he pulled her from the limo, her foot caught on the curb, throwing her off balance and right into his arms.

Lights flashed beside them but all he noticed was the way her bright green eyes locked onto his and the world fell away. Bart swallowed hard. How easy would it be for him to dip his mouth just a few inches lower and brush a firm kiss against those full lips?

More lights flashed and Izzie blinked before turning her attention to the side. And just like that she pulled away from him. Her hands trailed down her dress, straightening wrinkles that weren't present as a few people with cameras shouted out his name.

Right. He'd only found out about this auction due to his status. There were going to be a lot of local celebrities at this thing. He slipped his arm around her waist and leaned close to her ear. "I'm sorry. I forgot to warn you. There might be pictures."

Her body was no longer languid and soft. Instead, she remained stiff beside him, keeping her focus trained on the building. Another apology was on his lips but she finally spoke. "No. It's fine. I should have connected the dots. Even if we were to go anywhere local, there would be photogra-phers." She forced a smile. "I'll be fine."

He released her and found her hand instead. Bringing it up to his lips, he smiled at her again. "I'll be here with you every step of the way." Bart brushed a kiss to her hand and more flashes followed.

Izzie let out a little laugh. "The tabloids are going to have a heyday with this one. They're going to wonder what hole you dragged me out of."

Bart stopped, forcing her to step back to face him. "Don't disparage yourself, Izzie. You are just as beautiful as and probably a great deal stronger than all of those women. I would rather be wearing an ABBA t-shirt in your apart-ment with you than a fancy place like this with any of them."

Her laugh had to be the best thing he'd heard his entire life. It was something he'd never get tired of hearing. They entered through a pair of large glass doors. Overhead an oversized crystal chandelier glittered. The receiving room had several posters on easels showcasing what was up for auction. Everything from paintings to jewelry to high-end cars. Some of the items were displayed out in the open.

Everyone in the room was dressed to the nines, in tuxes and floor-length gowns. Izzie's demeanor shifted once again as she looked around the room, finding the guests staring at them. She seemed to scoot closer to him then suddenly she pulled him aside toward a part of the room where no one mingled. Her quiet voice was barely audible. "I really wish you would have told me to dress up nicer."

The corners of his mouth lifted. "Would you have come with me?"

"Probably not."

"Well, at least she's honest." He chuckled. "We're only

here for the necklace. As soon as we find out if it's the one, we'll be out of here. I have something better planned. I would never make you spend time with people who had *this much* money."

Izzie's hard features softened for just a moment and a hint of a smile tugged at her lips before she pulled them between her teeth. She looked from him to the people and back then nodded. "Okay. Let's track it down and get out of here."

He held out his hand and she stared at it for a moment before placing her own within his. He led them through the crowd, offering smiles to small groups of people he didn't recognize. Izzie might feel like she didn't belong here, but it was he who knew he wasn't made for this life. No matter how hard he tried, he hadn't been able to find his place.

Bart squeezed her hand, as if to reassure himself that she was still there. They stopped at various displays until they found the jewelry. Bart stood beside Izzie, allowing her time to look over the various pieces being presented.

The look of concentration on her face would have been cute if he wasn't so on edge about the whole thing. This was too important. Every so often she'd meet his gaze, offer a smile then shake her head. The more time they spent looking the more his stomach churned until he thought he might be sick.

An attendant moved through the parted crowd, holding a small pillow with something on top. He opened the display case and placed the silk cushion inside then locked it up again. Izzie released his hand and moved over to look at it.

Just by the way the light left her gaze, he knew.

It wasn't the right necklace.

Bart let out a disappointed sigh, the pressure in his

chest deflating like a popped balloon. He closed the distance between them and gazed at the necklace beneath the glass. It was a jade necklace. It probably had an inscription on the back. But it wasn't heart-shaped.

"I'm sorry," he murmured.

She gave him a watery smile. "Whatever for? This was the closest I've come to finding my mother's necklace. I wouldn't have passed up on this if you'd paid me to." She laced her fingers within his and rested her head against his shoulder. "It's a beautiful piece, but it's not my mother's necklace."

He tried ignoring her closeness. He desperately fought the way his body reacted to her touch. But the truth of the matter was he couldn't. Bart liked the way he felt when he was with her.

Izzie craned her neck around to look at him and grinned. "How about we blow this popsicle stand and do whatever it was you had planned?"

Bart grinned. "Our night is only going to get better. I guarantee it."

Chapter Thirteen

The ache in Izzie's chest lingered even after they climbed back into the limo. She'd allowed herself to get her hopes up. And everyone knew what went up had to come down. Bart had been wonderful. She still couldn't believe that he'd found an auction that had a necklace resembling the one her mother owned.

She eyed him as they sat in silence on their way to the next event. He wasn't anything like she'd expected him to be. Bart was far more down to earth and thoughtful than the majority of the guys she'd dated in the past.

He caught her staring at him and flashed her a smile. Izzie looked away, the heat in her face betraying her embarrassment. Her thoughts scrambled and tripped over all of the new information she had on him.

A teacher.

A man who could appreciate an old book.

A gentleman who knew how to listen.

Lump all those things together and add them to his new career path, his looks, and his personality—Bartholomew

Brown was a major catch. No wonder women practically threw themselves at him.

Surprisingly, he hadn't been snagged by even one of them—those sharks.

One afternoon with him, and they could smell blood in the water. They were circling and one of them would end up tricking him into falling in love with them. Heck, he was such a sweetheart, she wouldn't mind snagging him for herself.

She snorted, which turned into a cough. Izzie covered her mouth, attempting to suck in the oxygen her body desperately needed. Bart twisted toward her, concern etched in his face.

"Are you okay?"

Izzie nodded, her face probably turning even more red by the second.

Bart handed her a bottled water and she gratefully accepted. She refused to meet his gaze, knowing full-well that he could probably read her better than he ought to. Her embarrassment before was nothing compared to how she felt over her rogue thoughts.

As much as she agreed with the treacherous path her mind had taken her, it wasn't going to happen. Her life was a mess. Between her demanding job, caring for her mother, and tracking down that necklace, she didn't have time for a relationship.

Izzie tossed back the water Bart had given her and some splashed out. She took a deep breath and let out an embarrassed laugh. "Sorry about that."

"No apologies needed." His gaze dipped lower and he reached his hand toward her.

Izzie stiffened.

Bart brushed the knuckle of his finger against a spot just above her chin. His touch was soft and brief, but enough to stir something into life within her. His gaze lifted to meet hers. "You had a little water just there." His eyes bore into hers and that boyish grin returned to his face. He was so close, all she would have to do was lean toward him a couple inches and...

For heaven's sake, she needed to get her mind out of the gutter. Izzie scooted back into her seat, putting distance between them. She tucked a stray strand of hair behind her ear and shot a look in his direction. "Where are we headed now?"

The limo turned a corner and headed up what looked like a dirt road. They'd made it to the outskirts of town and it appeared they were headed toward a vineyard. She scooted closer to her door and stared out the window at the breathtaking landscape. Rolling hills of green, wildflowers, and of course the vines covered in fruit.

Her gaze swept back to Bart. "Are we going to a wine tasting?"

He shook his head. "Well, I suppose that's part of it. But no, it's not the big reason we're here."

Izzie's eyes narrowed.

"Just know that you have to take a chance on me."

"That's not cryptic at all."

He chuckled. "Knowing me... knowing you..."

"I feel like you're trying to give me hints but it's not working."

They turned around another bend and the faint sound of bass music came through the windowpane. Izzie glanced out the window. A large stage sat square in the middle of a large field. All around it people sat on blankets with picnic baskets. And a banner with four letters hung over the band setting up. Her eyes widened before she spun to face him. "Are we at an *ABBA* concert?"

"To be fair, they do covers of ABBA songs. They're not the real group."

She dragged her focus toward the stage again. This wasn't happening. It couldn't be. She had to be dreaming. Izzie turned around and faced him once more. "I don't believe it."

Confusion filled his expression. "What's not to get, they're right—"

"No. Not that. I can't believe you would go through all the trouble for this—for me." The last two words lowered to a whisper. "Why?"

He tilted his head, his unwavering stare putting her on edge like it had already done several times this evening. His quiet voice gave her shivers. "Why not?" He scrunched his mouth to one side. "Let me set something straight, Izzie. I wanted to ask you out because I thought you were interesting, beautiful, and exactly my type. When I'm interested in someone, I make sure they know. I could have chartered a plane or taken you to a fancy restaurant and showed off. But that's not who I am. And something tells me that isn't who you are either."

He'd hit that assumption right on. Back at the auction, she'd felt like a fish out of water. The only thing that had tethered her was Bart. Her instincts screamed that she shouldn't believe him. People weren't this candid or genuine.

Deep down she knew. Bart was different.

Her gaze dropped to her hands. "It's refreshing to meet someone who is less worried about showing off than he is about getting to know me. I'm actually impressed."

The limo door opened. Bart's lips twitched, lifting into a wide grin. "Shall we?"

Izzie nodded, letting him take her by the hand and helping her out of the vehicle. Here, they seemed to match the guests in their appearance and it wasn't difficult at all to find a place to settle and blend in.

Bart flicked their blanket out into the air and lifted it a few times until it floated to the ground like a piece of paper. Their driver seemed to have materialized with a picnic basket and Bart reached for it. He gestured toward the blanket. "Have a seat."

This all seemed so backwards. Bart wasn't supposed to be like this. She couldn't exactly keep hating him when every last shred of evidence was against her. Bart settled onto the blanket beside her and his arm brushed against hers. Izzie shivered.

"Are you cold?" he motioned toward their driver who spun around and darted toward the parking lot.

Her eyes widened and she shook her head. "He didn't have to do that. I'm fine, really."

Bart shrugged. "Just in case." He flashed her a smile that had her stomach knotting so bad she didn't think it would ever come untangled. She couldn't keep up with him.

The words he'd said to her in the limo came back to her and like a slap in the face, hit her hard. He was interested in her. Like ready to start dating interested in her. And for the first time in her life she didn't know what she should do. There was so much going on. Between her mother, her job, the necklace—she didn't have enough braincells to add a boyfriend to the mix. He had to understand that, right?

You need to relax a little. It's not like he was asking for your hand in marriage. You're overthinking all of it.

Izzie squeezed her eyes shut. It would be kind of nice, though. Bart was a decent guy. Would it be so bad if she were to give in a little and truly allow herself to let go? She was so exhausted all the time.

When she opened her eyes, he was staring at her, concern etched on his face. She let out a soft, strangled laugh and waved her hand through the air. "Don't worry. I'm just thinking."

"About what?"

Her face burst into color. There was no way to hide from it now. Bart leaned closer to her, his smile growing. "You can't leave me hanging like that Izzie. You're breaking a cardinal rule here."

"Oh really? And what rule is that?" She was stalling, she knew it and he did too.

Bart shifted even closer. His face came up right beside her ear and his warm breath fanned her neck. He lowered his voice so only she could hear. "I confessed something to you back in the car. Usually when such a confession is made, the other party then reciprocates."

Her mouth went dry and she had to clear it a few times before her voice would work again. "I said that you were refreshing, didn't I?"

He chuckled, a deep, throaty, rumble that sent chills coursing through her body. "You *know* that's not what I mean."

"What do you mean?" she whispered.

Bart pulled back. His eyes drilled into hers, then shifted to the side of her face. With soft fingertips, he brushed a strand of hair behind her ear. "I like you, Izzie. I can't say it any plainer than that."

"Okay," she murmured.

"Okay?" He tossed back his head and laughed. "Why did I think this would be even remotely easy?"

"Because you have money?" She uttered out the words before realizing what she'd said. Izzie clapped a hand on her mouth and shook her head. "Sorry. Habit." At least he didn't appear to be upset by the judgment.

Bart cocked his head the way he usually did when he seemed to be figuring something out. "I'll try one more time." He cleared his throat, and searched her face as he trailed the back of his hand along her jawline. "I like you Isobel Davis. And I want to date you. That being said, I'm not going to continue chasing something that doesn't want to be chased."

She blinked. No one had been that blunt with her before. No mind games.

"I don't expect an answer today or even this week. But if you come to a decision I want you to tell me. No hard feelings."

"I'm scared," she blurted.

His head pulled back with surprise.

"Not of you," she elaborated. "There's just a lot going on in my life right now. My mom. My job. All the stress of everything. I just don't know if you'd be happy in a relationship with me because—"

Bart's mouth closed in on hers. His lips roved against hers, searching, exploring with their soft texture. He clasped his hand against the nape of her neck and held her firmly, as if claiming her as his own.

She remained frozen at first, shocked. But then a glowing ember of desire, burst into a flicker. Izzie wrapped her arms around him and kissed him back. She was actually kissing billionaire Bartholomew Brown. The flame within her grew and warmed her whole body. What had she been so afraid of?

And just as quickly as it had started, it was over. Bart released her as he pulled away from her and looked off toward the stage. "I'm sorry," he murmured. "I shouldn't have done that." He peeked at her. "I told myself I wasn't going to do anything to jeopardize the trust developing between us."

It was like she'd been punched in the stomach. The air in her lungs whooshed out of her body and she felt light-headed. Though the latter might have been due to the breath stealing kiss Bart had just given her.

Izzie touched her still tingling lips, unsure of what to say. How could she tell him that only one kiss had been the thing to tip the scales?

Chapter Fourteen

Bart bit back a groan of displeasure. He'd tried so hard to make their date exactly what it was supposed to be to win her over. And he'd nearly made it until that moment.

Her words had been flying out of her mouth with such speed and anxiety that all he could think about was kissing her.

And it had been life-altering.

Dang it all.

He had one job—make her like him enough to go on another date, and then another. He was getting close, Bart could feel it. The fact of the matter was he'd messed everything up all because he couldn't control himself. By the way she just sat there in a daze, he knew it.

If this had been any other girl, he might have brushed it off. There were always additional means for changing the narrative. But Izzie was different.

Why wasn't she saying something—*anything*? Heck, even yelling at him would be better than being mute about the whole thing. If he could demand that she speak, he would. His whole body was on edge, waiting for the inevitable.

"Okay."

Bart stiffened. He could have sworn he heard her quiet voice, but the crowd was growing restless for the concert to start. Clearly, he'd imagined it. He peered at her over his shoulder. Izzie's green eyes stared back. She still touched her lips, but the shock seemed to have dissolved. She wasn't angry.

He twisted to face her. "What?"

Izzie opened her mouth then snapped it closed and gave him a firm stare. "Under one condition."

His mouth quirked up at the corners. "Of course there is."

It was clear she was biting back her own smile at this point. She looked away and peered at the sky where the sun was cresting behind the tree line. Once she appeared to have controlled herself, she met his gaze again. "I'm not some damsel in distress." Before he had even a chance to tell her he knew that already, she continued. "I don't want you saving me even if you think you know best."

"Why would I—"

"Like with the book. That was a sweet gesture—"

"That was a gift."

She gave him a pointed look. "As I was saying, that was a sweet gesture, but it was unnecessary. You have the means to fix almost any problem I might have and while I would appreciate it, I don't want you stepping in and messing with my life."

His features pinched. "How is helping you going to mess things up?"

Izzie sliced her hand through the air and shook her

head. "I know it's weird. You don't have to understand it. You just have to agree to my terms."

"Sure whatever you want."

Her face brightened into the most beautiful smile he'd ever seen. "Good."

Bart laughed. "Seriously? That's all you have to say?"

"Yep."

He laughed again, shaking his head. "Good," he repeated.

The tension in the air between them returned with a vengeance. He didn't know what he should do at this point. Was he supposed to hold her hand? Kiss her again?

Get it together, Brown. This is like any other relationship. Just enjoy yourself. Enjoy her company.

Simple. He could do that.

Bart pulled on the picnic basket handle, dragging it closer. He flipped open the lid and pulled out a few containers. There was one full of fruit, another with vegetables, two kinds of dips, and a cheese and cracker spread.

Izzie let out a low whistle. "Did you have your housekeeper prepare that for you?"

He shot her a disgruntled look. "No."

She shrunk back, chagrined. "Oh."

The smile that broke across his face rivaled hers from earlier. "My assistant put it together for me."

She whacked him with the back of her fingertips. "*Bart!*"

He chuckled again. "What?"

"You can't do that."

Bart plastered his most innocent expression on his face. "I can't do what exactly?"

"You know very well what."

He moved closer to her, slipping his arm around her waist and pulling her close. His lips brushed a trail of kisses along her jawline. "If you can tease me about my money, then I'd say embarrassing you about it is fair game," he murmured.

She sucked in a sharp breath and leaned her head away, giving him access to her neck. He placed one more kiss on her tender skin then rested his head against hers. "You know, money is just that. It's nothing special. It's what you do with it that makes you a good person or a bad person."

Izzie twisted around, pulling back enough that she could see his face. "I suppose you make a good point. Unfortunately, the majority of people who have a lot of it tend to use it to manipulate the world they live in to benefit only themselves."

"And there are those who refuse to work for it and demand that everything be handed to them. It's not a river —running in only one direction. Money issues are like a two-way street and people have to decide which side they're going to drive on."

Her whole body went very still. He wouldn't be surprised if her thoughts had shifted to her father and the decisions he'd made with their family's finances. He grimaced. Getting her to think about her father had not been his intention.

"That isn't to say that your father—"

She held up her hand. "You're right. He made his choices and showed his weaknesses. It wouldn't have mattered if he'd won the jackpot or even a million-dollar lottery. My father would have squandered every cent he got if given the chance." She glanced at him out of the corner of her eye. "Just like you could have kept every last penny your uncle gave you instead of doing something good with it." She dragged her gaze from his and focused on the food. Her fingers wrapped around a grape and she popped it in her mouth. After she'd swallowed, she took a deep breath. "I'm sorry."

"About what?"

She shrugged. "For judging you based on what I believed to be wrong with you."

"It's okay."

Izzie shook her head. "No, it's not. I needed to get past my prejudice." She forced a smile. "I'm just lucky you were willing to see through it and find the good in me."

He pulled her close again, not having the words to respond. Brushing his lips against the crown of her head, he marveled at how easily she'd come to this realization on her own. Humility like that wasn't common in today's generation.

He'd been right to be drawn to her. Isobel Davis was an angel—whether she could see it or not.

Bart laced his fingers within Izzie's as they headed up the cement pathway toward Maple Gardens. Today was the first day they were going to tell their family about their budding relationship. He didn't worry about his uncle as much as he did Izzie's mother. He wanted her to like him more than he'd wanted anything—except Izzie. He had a good feeling about her.

Margaret had liked him from day one, but then again, he hadn't been dating her daughter. It would be interesting to find out if her opinions would change.

"Ow."

He jumped and glanced at Izzie.

She held up their hands. "You don't have to squeeze so

hard." She tilted her head, her eyes dancing with humor. "Are you *seriously* that nervous about telling her?"

Bart lifted a shoulder. "So what if I am? She's your mother. You value her opinion. The last thing I need is for her to tell you I'm a no-good match for you and for you to kick me to the curb."

She laughed, a sound that both unnerved him and warmed him from the inside out. "Don't worry about my mom. She adores you."

He brought her hand up to his lips and kissed it. "I'm sure you're right. But let's just agree that the guys have it hardest when it comes to impressing the in-laws."

Izzie's brow arched. "In-laws?"

Heat crawled up his neck and filled his face. He wouldn't be surprised if there was steam rising off of him. "I mean, the *girlfriend's parents*."

"Um-hum," her voice was teasing, but it didn't do anything to quell the churning in his stomach. Talk about a Freudian slip if there ever was one. They'd only been dating for a couple weeks and already his mind was on marriage? That didn't seem right at all.

Or did it?

After they'd made it past that big hurdle, their relationship had been smooth sailing. He liked her friends and she was warming up to all the ways he liked to spoil her. As long as he didn't cross the line and do anything too big, she was happy.

And when she was happy, he was too.

They entered the building and walked up to the front counter. Olivia beamed at the two of them. "It's about time."

Bart glanced in Izzie's direction, noting the way her face blushed just as much as his had earlier. She hushed her friend and reached for the clipboard to sign in. "It's no big deal, Livy." But even as she said the words, her eyes met his and he knew better. She was just as thrilled as he was—and more so than Olivia.

Her friend rolled her eyes and leaned over the counter, resting her arms on the top. "Guess what Bart? Your uncle was talking this morning."

His eyes widened and he nearly dropped the clipboard that Izzie had handed him. "He was?"

Olivia's smile grew and she nodded. "Yeah. I mean, it wasn't much. And I wasn't there, but the nurses were talking about it."

"Do you know who was with him?" He shot a look in Izzie's direction and returned the sign-in sheet to the counter. "I have some questions for them."

Olivia dropped into her seat and turned to her computer. She stuck the tip of her tongue out and her brows furrowed. "It looks like Jenna and Tiff were on his schedule today. You could ask them."

Bart took a few steps away, then hurried back to Izzie's side. He kissed her cheek and let out a chuckle. "Don't tell her until I get there."

Izzie laughed. "I won't."

He kissed her again and hurried down the hall toward his uncle's room. There were nurses' stations set up in each wing of the building. If he was lucky, he wouldn't have to track anyone down. Hopefully Jenna or Tiff would still be on site. If they'd taken their lunch or their shift was over, he might lose his chance to speak with them.

Bart turned down the right corridor and came to a skidded stop at the nurses' station. A petite blonde woman glanced up from her computer and smiled at him. "Hi, Bart.

What can I do for you?" Her name tag read 'Susan' in bold, black lettering.

He glanced around the area but didn't see any other nurses readily available. "Do you by chance know if Jenna or Tiff are still here? I have a few questions to ask them."

Susan's brows furrowed and she stood to glance down the hallways leading to her desk. "I'm not sure. I thought I saw Tiff about an hour ago." She pulled her focus back to him. "Is there something I can do for you?"

He shook his head. "Not unless you were there when my uncle spoke this morning."

Susan frowned. "I'm sorry. I wasn't. My shift started about three hours ago. But I did hear about it. It was pretty exciting. When was the last time he spoke to anyone?"

"It's been a couple years," he admitted. "I wish I knew what set it off and what he said."

"Oh that's the strange thing," Susan returned to her seat, her eyes sparkling with mischief. "They didn't understand right away what he was trying to say, but then it started to make sense. We think he was asking for her."

He leaned toward her. "Who was he asking for?" He didn't have any children. The only person he could think of was his mother, but she didn't live in Georgia.

"Izzie. She's Margaret's daughter, right?"

His heart dropped into his stomach like a warm stone in water. "Yeah," he murmured. "She is."

Chapter Fifteen

Izzie pushed her mother's wheelchair down the hallway toward the doors that lead to the garden. She smiled politely at everyone they passed but her mind was on anything but manners. Her mother held the book Bart had given her in her lap.

How did she luck out and end up with a guy like him? The pessimist in her head insisted that there had to be something wrong with him. There were always things wrong with the perfect guys. Each and every one she'd dated had problems.

Okay, but Bart did have a few problematic issues. The casino was first and foremost the biggest. And he'd managed to persuade her to look past it. Doing so had turned out to be worth it.

The sunshine beat down on them as she wheeled her mother down the familiar paths they'd taken before. Her mother called out to people she knew and waved at them. The second they arrived at their favorite bench, Izzie settled onto the freshly lacquered wood and faced her mother. "Mom, I want to ask you something."

Her mother smiled. "Anything, dear."

She worried her lower lip between her teeth. Izzie had steered clear of conversations regarding her father. There had been too much pain and disappointment on that front. But the closer she got to Bart, the more she couldn't deny her thoughts had shifted. Her mother had been in love once. She probably thought that the man she married wouldn't hurt her.

In the end he had.

Izzie took a deep, shuddering breath. "Did you know about Dad's—issues—before marrying him?"

Margaret's brows furrowed. "What are you talking about?"

Lifting a shoulder, Izzie looked away. "I'm sure he was great. But most of what I remember isn't so much." Her cheeks blushed and she held back the emotion that threatened to spill from her eyes. "I guess I just wanted to know what he was like before..."

Her mother's pinched expression remained on her face.

It was short-lived, but for a second, Izzie was worried her mother's memory of her husband would be skewed because of the accident.

Margaret frowned and looked away. "I loved your father."

Izzie's heart constricted and she reached forward to rest a comforting hand on her mother's knee. "I know you did."

Her mother glanced at her, a bittersweet smile on her face. "I think he loved me. But sometimes there's something inside the people we love that doesn't come out until later."

Izzie's stomach knotted. That wasn't what she was hoping to hear. Her thoughts shifted toward Bart and the few things that had kept her away from him in the first place. How well did she really know him?

"What matters is if you love him. We all experience broken hearts, Izzie. It's like those characters in the books we read. Life is too short to let our worries hold us back. If you love someone, enjoy it."

Margaret's eyes seemed so clear and focused. Izzie hadn't seen this side of her since before the accident.

Leaning closer, Izzie whispered, "Why do you say that?"

Her mother blinked and looked away at something in the distance and when she brought her focus back to Izzie, it was once again clouded over with a haze of confusion. "What did you ask me Izzie? I seemed to have lost my train of thought."

"You were talking about falling in love."

Margaret shifted in her wheelchair and her brows furrowed. She mumbled something and shifted again. "I—I don't remember."

Izzie squeezed her mother's knee and straightened. "Its fine, Mom. Don't worry too much about it."

"There they are. See Uncle Larry, I told you we'd find them." Bart appeared, pushing his uncle in his wheelchair and smiling warmly at Izzie. But the second their eyes met, his features darkened. He must have read the ache or concern she had etched in her face. As much as she wanted to smile at him and show him everything was okay, it really wasn't.

She'd lost her mother again and at the moment she was feeling more lost than she could ever remember. For all intents and purposes, Bart seemed like the perfect guy for her. She could spend time with him and lose track of everything around her.

He made her happy.

Maybe what her mother had said held some truth. Life was too short to worry about what might happen. She needed to be willing to let go of the control she desperately sought after if she really wanted to be happy.

Bart settled onto the bench beside her and his arm draped along the back behind her. He leaned closer, "Is everything okay?"

She swallowed at the lump in her throat and nodded. "Yeah." Her voice wasn't at all convincing. She wouldn't be surprised if he pointed that out when they were alone. Instead he shifted his focus to her mother and offered her his most charming smile. "How are you today, Ms. Davis?"

Her mother's features immediately brightened as she smiled at him. "Oh I'm just lovely. How are you?"

Bart's gaze bounced from Margaret to his uncle then landed on Izzie. "Today is a pretty good day. Izzie and I wanted to tell you something exciting."

Margaret's eyes cut to Izzie. "Is that so?"

Bart lifted his hand from behind Izzie and reached for the one she held in her lap. A tingling sensation trailed up Izzie's arm from his touch and warmed her heart. Her fears were silly. She'd found a total catch and she wasn't about to do anything to jeopardize it. Margaret crooned as her eyes landed on their clasped hands. "Oh I just knew something was going on between the two of you." She leaned forward and held onto Izzie's free hand. "You know I have a sense for these things. You two make a lovely couple. Don't they, Lawrence?" She glanced at Bart's uncle.

The man's eyes shifted from staring off into space to Bart. At least that's how it appeared. He mumbled something, causing Bart to jolt from his seat and move close to his uncle.

Izzie jumped, her wide eyes shifting from Lawrence to Bart. "Did he just say something?"

Bart shot a look over his shoulder toward her. "Apparently he spoke earlier today as well."

Izzie gasped. "What did he say?"

Lawrence mumbled again, but this time it was clearer. "Iz...zie."

Her mouth dropped open. She had to have imagined it. Why would he say *her* name?

Bart laughed and looked toward her again. "You heard that, right? Please tell me I'm not hearing things."

"I—"

"I heard it clear as day," Margaret beamed as she grasped Lawrence's hand within her own. She turned her smile to Izzie. "He must approve of your relationship too. You make such a handsome couple."

She was pinned between both her mother's and Bart's gaze. A swirl of strange emotions filled her chest. The worry was still there but had taken a back seat to the happiness she'd felt earlier and that blended with the awe of Lawrence's muttered word.

What could she say? None of this made sense and at the same time it made perfect sense. Izzie met Bart's gaze and nodded. "I think so too, Mom."

———

Izzie took a deep breath as she stood outside the casino. She had never stepped foot inside a casino—places like this made her sick to her stomach. As if on cue, her insides roiled. A group of guys who looked to be about college age laughed, brushing past her as they headed inside.

She jumped out of the way, stumbling to take a few

steps back. Why was this so hard? It's not like she was liter-ally traumatized by being inside one of these places. Her father had been the one to visit and take with him every-thing that was important in her life.

Shaking her head, she took a few more steps backward until she was out of the path from visitors coming and going. If Bart wanted her to come visit, he'd have to escort her inside. She turned from the building and made her way toward a bench that was situated beneath some trees. She dialed his number and held her phone to her ear.

"Izzie?" Bart's warm voice only helped put her slightly at ease. "Are we still on for lunch today?"

Izzie nodded then flushed. He couldn't see her. "Yes. But there's a problem."

"What's wrong?" Immediately his voice went tight. She could almost imagine him standing from his desk, ready to come help get her out of any trouble she might find herself in. "Do you need help?"

She let out a strangled laugh. The irony of that question was almost too much. Swallowing hard, Izzie's focus shifted toward a man, obviously drunk, wandering out of the casino. Her whole body tightened, her head spun and she had to close her eyes to steady herself. "I don't think I can come inside."

There was silence for only a moment but clearly no hesitation. "I'll come to you."

He arrived outside faster than he should have. Then again, she didn't know what floor his office was on. He probably had easy access to the exit. Bart strode toward her and swept her into his arms. "I'm sorry. I didn't even think about what it might mean for you to come here. I should have—"

She shook her head and let out another nervous laugh. "I don't even know why I'm stressing so much about it."

Bart stepped back. He hooked his finger under her chin, forcing her to look at him. "You went through a trauma. Anything related to that trauma is going to be hard to work through. Even if it's entering a building that stands for everything you hate." He searched her gaze, as if looking for proof that she accepted his words.

Stunned.

That was the only thing that registered in her mind. She was absolutely stunned by his support. He could have coaxed her to come inside by telling her that he'd be there in the elevator. He could have come out and insisted she was being ridiculous and that they go inside.

But no. Bart wanted her to know that he understood her.

Izzie threw her arms around his neck, rubbing her nose against his chest. "I love you."

He went still.

She froze.

Every part of her body heated as if she'd caught on fire.

No. No. No. No. No.

She couldn't have said that. Please, anything but that.

Bart was the first one to move. He disentangled her arms from his neck, held her by her upper arms, and pushed her away just enough for him to see her face.

Izzie squeezed her eyes shut, unable to fight the mortifying blush that had covered her from head to toe. They hadn't been dating long enough to warrant saying those words. It had been instinct. Or something else.

But something nagged at her. Maybe she *did* feel it.

"Isobel," he whispered.

She dragged her eyes open and met his inquisitive gaze.

Her throat was dry and her tongue felt like it was made of lead. She couldn't speak. There was no excuse she could say to make this better.

It would be easy to predict what was about to happen. Bart would tell her that he cared about her but he wasn't ready for something that serious. She'd laugh it off and agree with him. She hadn't meant to say it. She should probably beat him to it.

"I—" she started.

He placed a finger on her lips. "I love you too."

Chapter Sixteen

Bart hadn't expected Izzie to confess anything to him—let alone a proclamation of love. His mind hadn't even considered such things. But when she said those three little words, his entire world was tipped on its side and there was no denying it.

He'd fallen for her and he'd fallen hard.

Isobel Davis was the kind of girl he'd do anything for.

Bart pulled her close again. Words were trite and even if he knew what to say to her, he would probably stumble over every single phrase. Besides, he wasn't about to let her brush anything aside. She was in love with him and he was in love with her.

Everything around them faded. The people coming and going from the casino. The breeze rustling through the trees overhead. Her heartbeat beating in time with his own—that's what grounded him.

They sat like that for what felt like hours but in reality was only a few minutes. Finally Izzie pulled back and gazed at him. She blinked a few times, that beautiful blush making her green eyes even more pronounced. "Okay, so that just happened."

Bart chuckled, tipping her chin up so he could get a better look at her. "Yeah."

"What does that mean—for us?"

"What do you want it to mean?"

She smiled, her eyes darting away even though he held her chin steady. "I don't know. I guess I'm just happy to be dating you."

"Me too."

Her gaze flitted to meet his once more. "And I guess I'm glad I found someone who understands me like you do—who doesn't ask me to be something I'm not."

"You're pretty lucky."

Izzie gasped and slugged him in the arm. "And you're not humble at all."

He shrugged. "That's to be expected, right? Because I have money?" he teased.

Her blush deepened but she didn't pull away. "I was wrong."

Bart arched a brow. This was an interesting turn of events. "Oh?"

"You're nothing like I expected, Bart. Yes, you have money. But you don't use it like people expect you to. You're down to earth and you have these morals that make you —different."

He chuckled. "I hope that's a compliment."

"Oh, it is." She lifted her hand to his cheek, placing her palm against his skin and setting off a domino of chills down his spine. "I am lucky that you were stubborn enough to win me over."

Bart leaned into her warm touch. "No, I'm the lucky one."

They ended up walking down to a local food truck and ordering tacos for lunch. Then Izzie went her way and he returned to his office. Things couldn't have gone more perfect today if he'd paid some higher power to set it all in motion. They were quickly following a path that could lead them to something much more.

Marriage?

He shoved aside the thought. They'd only just confirmed their feelings for one another. He shouldn't push his luck.

Even still...

One day he would like to discuss the possibility with her. He'd never been the bachelor type and his inheritance had inhibited any progress he'd made on the relationship front. Izzie's aversion to his wealth was only part of it. Usually women flocked to him so they might get something out of it.

Thank heavens he'd found someone who preferred to live modestly. His uncle had married several times, but each time it had been to a woman who only wanted what he could provide her with—lavish gifts and high society. In the end Lawrence had ended up alone like scrooge himself.

Now as he stood in his uncle's office staring down at the courtyard that surrounded the casino, he couldn't help but wonder what might have happened with his uncle if he'd found his own Izzie. Women like her were one in a million.

He wanted to do something for. She'd never ask for anything, so he'd have to come up with something on his own. Bart paced his office. There had to be something he could do for her that she would appreciate. It should be thoughtful and something she actually needed.

Rubbing his jaw, he paused in the center of his office, completely stumped. He could get her groceries. No, that might be embarrassing. Her apartment was small and he could help her find a new place, maybe subsidize her rent. Okay, that was worse. She'd hate him pushing such a big change on her.

"Sir?"

His head whipped up and he glanced at his secretary standing in the doorway. "What is it?"

"The event and marketing coordinator is here to help you plan for that karaoke night."

"I'll be right there."

She nodded and slipped from the room.

He hadn't gone into too much detail about his karaoke plans with Izzie, due to the way she reacted about entering the casino. Heck, she might not even be interested. However, with how much she liked singing, perhaps she'd change her mind eventually.

If only she still had her guitar.

Bart snapped his fingers.

That's it.

He could get her a guitar to replace the one she lost. Izzie wouldn't be able to refuse a gift like that. It was practical and it was something she'd lost. Of course he would have liked to find that jade necklace Izzie had lost, but at this point he didn't know if it would make an appearance at all within the next several years.

He shrugged on his suit jacket and secured the top button then headed out of his office. He'd make a quick stop to the guitar shop in downtown and if they didn't have what he was looking for, he'd order it. He couldn't wait to see the way her eyes lit up when she saw it.

It had taken a few different trips to various instrument shops in town for Bart to realize that the guitar he wanted for Izzie wasn't readily available. It had to be perfect—top of the line. And it had to be something that would just fit in her hands like they were meant to be with each other.

His search turned to online vendors. He couldn't use any of the big box stores. No, he had to go with a specialty vendor and the guitar he'd finally found was made to order. It had arrived today, and it was literally one of a kind.

He'd managed to find someone who could construct a Martin OM-45 Deluxe with rosewood and Adirondack then accent the top with a jade inlay. It wasn't the jade necklace she was searching for, but maybe it would be something she could play and think of him as she did so.

Bart hadn't unwrapped it yet. It was still in a shipping box in his office. At this point he was planning on having Izzie do the unveiling at her place when he came to pick her up for their date. He was almost as excited as he'd been when he was a kid on Christmas morning and he wasn't even getting anything.

When the workday was done, he lumbered up to her apartment with the box in hand. He couldn't wait for her to see her reaction. He'd never worked this hard to pick out a gift for someone.

He leaned the box against the wall and pressed the doorbell. Footsteps tapped through the apartment and hurried to the door. Izzie opened it, the gust of air that came with the door tugged at her tendrils of hair that framed her face. She flashed him a smile and motioned for him to come inside. "I have a few more things to do and then I'll be ready."

Bart grabbed the box just as she turned and moved through her apartment toward her room. He brought the package inside and shut the door, then leaned it against the door.

"I hope we won't miss our reservation," she called, "Will they give it to someone else if we're too late?" Her voice drifted through the apartment as he wandered toward the couch and took a seat.

"I don't think so. It's just at that new gourmet burger place down the street."

She appeared in the hallway. The deep green sundress she wore made her eyes pop. He launched from his seat, his mouth hanging open. Izzie let out a soft laugh. "What?"

"You look—wow." He gestured toward his polo shirt and khakis. "I feel severely underdressed."

Izzie brought her hands up to put in a pair of earrings. "You look as handsome as ever. I just thought I'd dress it up a little bit." Her eyes drifted toward the larger than life package that rested against the door, then shot to meet his. "What's that?" Her tone shifted from happy to almost accusatory.

"I got you a little something."

"Bart," she warned, "that's not little."

He shrugged. "I was just thinking about you and I wanted to get you something nice."

Her shoulders relaxed slightly even as she eyed the gift with caution. "That's sweet of you, but—"

"You'll understand when you open it. I've been working on this new thing at the casino..."

Izzie had moved across the room and was unwrapping the guitar as he blabbered on.

"I figured maybe at some point you'd—"

She gasped.

Bart moved closer, grinning from ear to ear as she stared speechless at the guitar in all its glory. "Do you like it?" He slipped an arm around her waist and pulled her close to press a kiss to her temple.

Izzie didn't move for a few minutes. She was completely awestruck. That's exactly what he had wanted. He'd picked the perfect gift and she had no words.

"Take it back."

"I knew you'd—wait, what?"

She shrugged away from him and stalked across the room. "I said take it back. I don't want it."

His head whipped around to watch her disappear into the hallway. "But—I thought you—Isn't it—" He spun on his heel and charged after her. "Izzie, wait." He leaped over the coffee table and headed down the hall after her.

Izzie darted into a bedroom and he finally managed to catch up to her. When he touched her shoulder, she whirled around, her eyes flashing. "How could you?"

He took a short step back, confusion and even a little guilt flooded his consciousness. Why was he feeling guilty? He hadn't done anything wrong. "How could I what?"

She poked his chest. "You know I don't like it when you spend money like that on me. Why would you do that?" The pain in her voice didn't match the fury in her eyes.

"Okay, let's back up a little. You're upset because I got you a present?"

Izzie threw her hands in the air. "It's like you don't know anything about me."

"But I got you that guitar because I thought you'd like it."

She let out a sound that resembled a growl. "I *love* it."

He rubbed the back of his neck, his head was beginning to hurt. "Then why do you want me to take it back?"

Izzie scowled at him. "You can't spend that kind of money on me."

"Why the heck not?" his voice rose slightly. "You're my girlfriend and I love you. I should be allowed to do what I want."

Her mouth dropped open. "Do you even hear yourself? I said I didn't want it, so take it back. This isn't about you. It's about our relationship. You know how I feel about you dropping unnecessary money on gifts for me. Remember the book?"

His brows creased. But he'd bought the book before they were dating. Their relationship had changed. This shouldn't be a problem.

Izzie sighed. "I appreciate the thought, Bart. I really do. But when you do stuff like that, it makes me uncomfortable."

"It shouldn't."

She squeezed her eyes shut and let out another measured breath. When she opened her eyes, she set a firm gaze on him. "When you're in a relationship with someone you have to respect their wishes. I thought you understood that."

Her words sliced through him, but more so was the fact that she had refused the gift he'd worked so hard to procure for her. His jaw tightened. "Fine. If you don't want it, don't have it." He pivoted and exited her room. At this point going to dinner would be more awkward than cancelling the reservation.

By the looks of it, she wasn't interested in going out anymore either.

Bart gathered up the packaging and the guitar and left her apartment without a word.

Chapter Seventeen

Izzie moved across her room and slumped down on the edge of her bed. She'd lost her appetite the second she saw the guitar. It really was perfect. The jade accents had drawn her eye and the craftsmanship was next level.

The fact remained that he couldn't just do stuff like that. Money was important and should only be spent on necessities. She fully intended on replacing the guitar she had to pawn to pay for her mother's care. But never would she pick something so obviously out of reach financially.

She knew instruments far better than he probably gave her credit for. That guitar he'd bought wasn't some off-the-shelf, dime-a-dozen manufactured piece. That guitar was custom made. Her chest hurt just thinking about how she had to put her foot down and help him understand where she was coming from. Hopefully he finally realized that there were other ways to show love.

The front door slammed shut and the apartment grew quiet.

So much for a nice evening out with the man she loved. She dropped back on her bed and stared at the ceiling.

Something tickled down her face and she brushed at it. When she pulled her hand away, she found it wet.

Great. Now she was crying. This wasn't their first argument, but it had was the hardest. Deep down she had wanted to jump up and down and throw her arms around his neck to tell him how excited she was for this present. But even the thought of doing that made the churning in her stomach worsen.

Izzie squeezed her eyes shut, forcing another tear to trickle down the side of her face. She refused to feel guilty over her request. What she really needed to do was get out of this apartment and stop moping about their fight.

Bart would come to his senses and apologize. She'd probably apologize too, and they'd move on.

Izzie sat up, her eyes sweeping through the room for her phone. There was one person she could count on to drop everything for her.

Olivia.

She got up from the bed and headed into the kitchen, looking for the device until she finally found it on the coffee table. Beside the phone was a small envelope with her name scrawled over the top. Bart must have forgotten to grab it when he left.

As much as she wanted to read it, she couldn't. Not with the way she'd refused his gift. Izzie grabbed a nearby book and placed it on the envelope, hiding it from view. Then she retrieved her phone and dialed her friend. She needed a night out more than anything and someone to tell her she had made the right decision.

"You're wrong, Izzie."

Izzie coughed on the sip of soda she'd just put in her mouth. "*What?*"

Olivia shrugged. "Guys buy girls gifts all the time. If Bart wants to get you a guitar, you accept graciously."

She shook her head. "No. You're wrong."

Her friend laughed. "*No*, I'm not. Think about it Izzie. From the beginning of time, it's what the guys do to win over a girl's affection. Heck, even some animals do it."

Izzie huffed, folding her arms and looking into the crowd of people dancing in the middle of the room.

"I mean it, Izzie. I think penguins find pebbles for their mates. It's not uncommon at all."

"I didn't say it was uncommon, Olivia," she groaned. "I said he knew I didn't like stuff like that and he did it anyway."

Olivia arched a manicured brow and leaned back in her seat as she folded her arms. "Are you sure he didn't know?"

"Well..." Maybe he didn't. No—he had to. "When he tried to give me that book—"

"That book doesn't count. You weren't dating then. He just wanted to give you something because he wanted to. There was no quid pro quo about it."

Izzie gasped. "Well, there certainly isn't any quid pro quo about the guitar either, if that's a qualifying measure."

"You're making my point for me." Her friend laughed again. "This is Bart we're talking about. The most eligible bachelor in the entire state. He's got more money than he knows what to do with. He could have blown several thousands of dollars on you and gotten you a car."

"I'm pretty sure that guitar cost more than my car."

Olivia threw her hands in the air. "That's not the point I'm trying to make." Frustration edged her voice. "Bart is a catch—like the best guy you could have ever dreamed of dating. He actually thought out the perfect gift for you and you threw it back in his face. I'm sorry, Izzie, but this time you are wrong."

"But—"

"I'm not saying you have to ask for him to give it back to you. I'm not even suggesting that you have to keep it if he were to try offering it again. All I want to emphasize is one thing. Is this the mountain you want to die on?" Olivia's eyes peered at her with a ferocity that sent a chill down Izzie's back.

She looked away, not feeling the least bit comfortable about the way it felt like her friend was staring into her soul. "What is that supposed to mean anyway?"

"What if Bart thinks you don't want him anymore?"

Her head whipped around and she gaped at Olivia. "He wouldn't think that."

Olivia shrugged and pulled out one of her hands as if to examine her fingernails. "All I know is if I were you, I wouldn't be so stubborn. I'd call him up and tell him I'm sorry for my outburst and try to explain to him in a way he understands that I don't want him spending his money on me.—if I were you." Her eyes flicked up to meet Izzie's again. "But seriously, what woman wouldn't want that? I'm beginning to think you might be a little crazy after all."

"You *know* why," Izzie muttered.

Olivia sighed and leaned across their small table. She grasped Izzie's hand and squeezed it. "Yeah. I get it. Money has always been a big deal in your family. If your dad hadn't royally messed you up by stealing everything you had and throwing it away, I don't think this would be a big deal."

"Maybe, maybe not. Honestly, I think I'd feel the same way. I take pride in what I have and that I've earned it.

Everything I can claim as my own—no one else can say they were responsible."

Olivia squeezed her hand once more. "I know."

As much as she hated to admit it, Izzie knew Olivia had a point. But only on the communication part. Just because Bart wanted to spend money didn't mean he had the right to do it the way he wanted to. This relationship they had was something between the two of them. That mean he needed to understand and respect the boundaries she'd set out.

She sighed and took another sip of her soda. That mean the two of them would have to have another strained discussion. This argument wasn't going to be fixed if she didn't lay out in clear terms what she needed from him.

Dang it, why did relationships have to be so complicated? He should have known when he'd tried giving her that book, for heaven's sake.

But it was like Olivia pointed out. This fight wasn't worth losing him over. She wasn't about to be a push over and let him keep on doing something she didn't approve of, but she wouldn't call it quits when they hadn't had a chance to come to a common understanding.

She'd let them both cool off before she attempted that discussion. For now, she wasn't about to waste a perfectly good evening with her best friend. Izzie nodded to Olivia then gestured around them at all the people dancing and mingling. This club wasn't like some of the more seedy ones they'd been to in the city. It was actually nice. The music was loud but not so bad they couldn't carry on a conversation. People were cut off early enough that there were few if any drunken mishaps. It was the perfect place to decompress with Olivia.

Olivia looked around the room then set a questioning gaze on Izzie. "What?"

"Are you going to find anyone fun to dance with? Or are you going to sit with me all night?"

She shrugged. "I don't know. I think I might be over this whole dating thing. Did I tell you that I met someone last week who was a complete narcissist?"

Izzie shook her head. "What happened?"

"He literally bumped into me at the coffee shop by my work—spilled his iced coffee all over me."

Izzie's eyes widened. "You didn't tell me anything about that."

"Well, instead of apologizing and telling me he'll get me a new shirt—you know, like they do in all the movies—he scowls at me and demands to know why I was in his way."

"Well, were you?"

She sliced her hand through the air dismissively. "Does it matter? Just because I might be in the way doesn't give him the right to bump into me and then blame me. Normal people go around."

Izzie bit back a smile. This wasn't funny, but it was also Olivia. She was probably on her phone or daydreaming about something. "Okay, so I'm assuming there's more to this story than you're letting on."

Olivia nodded. "I was taking over a shift for one of the girls. You know how I never work Sundays."

Izzie nodded as well. "Yeah."

"Okay, so I go to the bathroom and attempt to clean up my shirt before heading to work. I can't be late otherwise they're going to have me come in for a disciplinary meeting." She rolled her eyes. "I've already been late too many times this year. Anyway, when I come out of the bathroom, he's gone. Good riddance. Well, I head to work and who do I end up bumping into?"

Izzie's mouth dropped open. "You bumped into him again?"

"Not literally. But yeah. Mr. Narcissist is there at Maple Gardens visiting his mom or his aunt or someone."

"What did you do?"

"What *could* I do? I'm not going to lose my job over getting into it with a client's family member."

Izzie snickered. "Since when did you make that a rule?"

Olivia offered her a chagrinned smile. "Okay, I won't get into it with client's family *anymore*."

"Honestly, I don't know why you keep working there if you don't like it."

"What makes you think I don't love it?"

She gave Olivia a pointed look.

Olivia laughed. "Yeah, okay. I know I complain more than I should. But I really do love working there. It's just that sometimes people can be so dumb."

"Tell me about it." Her thoughts shifted to Bart and their current predicament.

"Anyway, if I end up bumping into that guy again, I don't know what I'll do. Maybe I'll dump my coffee on *him*."

"Olivia," Izzie laughed, "you wouldn't."

"I might. Especially if he's all dressed fancy like he was that day. He's probably some businessman."

"You didn't even look him up?"

Olivia shook her head. "Why would I? I don't want to date him. He's not my type—besides the fact that he is super attractive." She wagged her eyebrows. "But seriously, I'm not in the market for a guy who doesn't have manners. If I ever see him again, you can rest assured I will walk the other way, and fast."

"Speaking of dating, is there anyone you're interested in?"

"Why, do you know anyone?"

Izzie's lips puckered then her eyes widened and a smile filled her face. "No, but I bet Bart knows some guys. With the circles he's running in, you might be able to find an eligible bachelor of your own."

"Maybe. But first you fix whatever is wrong with your relationship." There was only a veiled interest in Olivia's eyes. But it was enough that when this whole problem with Bart was settled, she knew exactly what they would be doing. Olivia deserved happiness more than anyone she knew. And it would be fun to find someone who got along with Bart so they could double.

"Deal."

Chapter Eighteen

Bart fumed as he paced in his office. He'd managed to keep his cool long enough to make it behind his office door before he felt the urge to punch something. Then he had to remind himself that getting angry wasn't going to make anything better.

The guitar rested against the wall, mocking him. It stared at him as if to say he was an utter failure. He should have known she wouldn't want something so ostentatious. All he had to do was look around her apartment and acknowledge that she didn't own anything expensive. Heck if she'd kept the guitar, it would be the most valuable item she owned.

He pinched the bridge of his nose as he came to a stop near the large window of his office. His eyes were squeezed shut tight but it did nothing to ward off the embarrassment and guilt he felt over doing something so *stupid*. He should go over there and apologize.

No, not yet. He couldn't smother her.

Bart looked over at the guitar once more. Deep inside, he knew it belonged to her. It was perfect for her. But the only way he'd be able to give it to her is if she came to her senses and accepted it.

No, he admonished himself once more. Izzie was allowed to have her own opinions on what kinds of gifts she wanted.

He let out a deep sigh.

Well, there was no way he was going to return it even if there was a return policy. Maybe one day he'd be able to find a way to ask her if she'd like to have it rather than spring it on her like the terrible surprise it was.

There was a quiet knock on the door and it opened on silent hinges. Isaac's familiar face appeared in the doorway. "I didn't realize you'd be here. I was just going to drop off some documents for you to sign." His brows creased. "Did I catch you at a bad time?"

Bart shook his head and held out his hand. "Don't be absurd. I'll sign them now."

Isaac held a file out to Bart as he slipped into the office and shut the door behind him. He moved across the room and settled into a chair. "Looks like you're having a rough day. Is the job finally getting to you?"

Bart glanced up at his friend from over his files. "Hmm? What? No, that's not it." He signed his name on the first document then flipped to the other. "It's Izzie," he murmured as he scanned the next document. All the paperwork had to do with the donations he was giving to Maple Gardens. Where money would be allocated and what it would cover. Margaret came to the forefront of his mind and his gut instinct was to mention some of the profits ought to go to her accounts.

But that would probably only make Izzie more upset with him.

"That's the girl you're dating, right?"

He nodded, signing the next document. "I got her a present and she refused."

Isaac laughed. "You're kidding."

Bart glanced at his friend and shook his head. "I'm not. She has this strange obsession with money." He let out a sigh. "That's not fair—and to be honest, it's totally understandable with what she had to deal with as a kid." He settled into his chair and leaned back, studying Isaac. "Are you dating anyone?"

Isaac shook his head. "Where would I find the time? Honestly? I want to know your secret. You have just about as much on your plate as I do."

He shrugged. "I suppose I make time for what I find important." And Izzie was about the most important part of his life right now.

"Well, as much as I'd like that kind of connection, I think most women these days have a little bit of crazy in them. It's best if we just let them domesticate themselves first." He chuckled.

"Maybe you just haven't met the right one."

"Perhaps."

They sat like that for a few minutes, each trapped within their own thoughts. Izzie needed to feel like she could trust him. If that meant making sure she didn't feel triggered from her past, he could do that. Eventually she might trust him enough to let him do things for her. But right now, he would try harder to be the man she needed. Isaac cleared his throat and Bart dragged his focus back to the present.

"Whatever it is you're dealing with—I know you'll figure it out. You always do."

Isaac's compliment warmed him, giving him the small amount of peace he needed to get through this evening without calling Izzie. After they each let their frustrations settle, they'd be able to find their common ground. They always did.

Isaac shuffled through the paperwork and paused. He held up a document. "You didn't fill this one out completely."

Bart eyed the document. "I'm still working out the details on that one."

His friend's brows furrowed. "For how the money donated to Maple Gardens is going to be dispersed?"

Bart nodded. "I haven't decided if I'm going to have the administrators allocate the funds where they feel is best, or if I'm going to award individual residents."

Isaac's gaze flitted toward Bart, a wry smile on his face. "I see."

"What?" Bart fought the urge to release yet another sigh.

"Does this have something to do with the mother of a certain someone?"

"So what if it does? It's my money to donate. I can decide where it goes."

Isaac stacked his papers together and shrugged, that stupid smile still on his face. "I never said you couldn't. I don't think anyone would dare tell you how to spend your money." He rose from his chair and stuck his folder under his arm. "Don't take too long deciding what you want to do. I don't like having anything in limbo." He turned and strode toward the door then stopped and glanced at Bart over his shoulder. "Maybe when things settle down, we can do a double date."

"But I thought you didn't have a girlfriend."

"I don't. But I'm sure Izzie has friends, right? Maybe it's time I take some pointers from you and prioritize something other than work. I'll see you later, Bart. Good luck with Izzie."

Left alone with the guitar in the corner and no one to speak to, Bart felt the shadows creeping in on him again. It was too quiet. His irritation regarding the gift he'd given her still smarted just beneath the surface—not enough to cause him to march back to her apartment and demand she accept it.

But enough that he didn't know if he'd be able to keep his cool if she were to be the next one to walk into his office.

Bart grabbed his suit coat from where it rested on a chair. His whole body hummed with an energy he couldn't seem to control. Maybe he needed to take up running again.

It wasn't that he was trying to stay away, but Bart found himself avoiding any confrontation with Izzie. There was something deep inside him that still couldn't agree with her opinion on gift giving.

If he were honest with himself, he'd admit that it felt like Izzie was doing the same thing. They were no longer in sync. Both of their schedules didn't seem to line up as easily. They still spoke on the phone, but it had been just over a week since he'd seen her in person, where before it had been nearly every day even if it was just for coffee.

Bart sat at a table across from his uncle at Maple Gardens. The only reason he'd made certain to visit was because he owed it to Lawrence. His uncle had given him everything he had now. And Bart was all Lawrence had.

His uncle stared off in a daze across the field. Bart studied the man's worn features. He wasn't terribly old. If his mind hadn't failed him, he would have still been in charge of all of his holdings. Instead, he was alone. Bart swallowed hard. He'd always wondered why Lawrence hadn't married.

"You're such a good son."

He jumped and turned to find that Isaac's mother had approached. He offered her a smile. "We've been through this, Millie. I'm Lawrence's nephew."

She scoffed, waving at him dismissively. "You are as much his son as Isaac is mine." Millie pulled out a chair from their table and settled beside him. "Do you honestly think he would have left everything to you if he didn't think of you as such? You mean more to him than you will ever know." She grinned and reached out to squeeze his hand. "And you fill the role fabulously."

"Thanks," he murmured.

Her eyes crinkled at the edges. "I've noticed that this week you haven't been coming with your girlfriend. Izzie. She's Margaret's daughter."

His chest twinged and set his focus on his uncle instead of Millie's probing stare. "It's been hard making our schedules work."

Millie shifted but didn't say anything right away. An RN wandered past with one of the residents and his gaze followed them until they left his view.

"You know, I think Lawrence has missed seeing her. He sure likes her."

"Yeah, I know." The guilt twisted inside him like a tangled ball of wire.

"I hope everything is okay. We've been rooting for you two."

His eyes finally swung over to meet hers. "We?"

She nodded, her smile widening. "There's a couple of us." Millie lowered her voice conspiratorially. "Don't you breathe a word, but we've been betting on who will end up together."

His brows pulled together and he shook his head. "You're doing what?"

Millie laughed. "Honey, Maple Gardens might be one of the better places to live when we can't care for ourselves on our own any longer. But it can still get boring. And many of us have children who are so wrapped up in work that they haven't found someone special to be with." She blew out a breath. "Isaac is *so* stubborn in that respect. I've tried having him ask out several girls who come here to visit their family and he flat out refuses."

The edges of Bart's mouth twitched as he fought his growing smile. "So there's a group of you, huh?"

Her cheeks seemed to pink up a little, but out of excitement more than embarrassment. "There's me, Alice and Lily. And to be honest, we've been enthralled with watching you and Izzie. Of course we haven't spoken to Margaret about our little obsession. I don't know if she'd be too keen on our little hobby." She let out a little laugh. "But let me tell you, if the two of you don't work out—or even if you do —we're going to have to find another way to stay busy."

"Well, I'm glad we could provide you with some kind of entertainment." This conversation had quickly turned awkward, especially with the tumultuous state of his relationship with Izzie.

"Oh you have! And I'm so glad that you are taking this so well." She shifted in her seat and glanced around the courtyard before bringing her focus back to him. "So, now that you know, I was curious if you could talk to Isaac."

He stilled. "Talk to him about what?"

"About being open to relationships. Were you even listening? We fancy ourselves matchmakers and Isaac is the first on our list. He needs a sweet girl like Izzie. So can you help him see how important a strong relationship is?"

"With all due respect, Millie. I can't convince Isaac of anything. You know that better than anyone."

She sighed. "But you're his friend. He would listen to you. That's all I need, we'll do the rest. Like putting the perfect girl in his path."

Bart snorted. "It's going to take a lot more than just talking to him. He'll be ready when he's ready."

Millie gave him a smile that almost appeared condescending. "Honey, sometimes you boys don't know what's good for you until you practically trip over it. Isaac needs a little shove in the right direction and then he'll be happy just like you."

If this was happiness, Bart needed to do something about it. He needed to settle things with Izzie before they grew more distant. "Okay. Sure, I'll mention it."

Her smile brightened. "Wonderful." Millie stood and squeezed his shoulder this time. "It was a pleasure speaking with you, Bartholomew. Thank you for your help."

His eyes followed her as she moved through the courtyard. Her words had only solidified one thing. He needed to do something fix things with Izzie.

Something small.

Chapter Nineteen

She wasn't being stubborn. At least that was what Izzie was trying to convince herself of. No, they hadn't broken up so she didn't have anything to settle. Bart hadn't come by her apartment for the last week because he was busy.

So why did she feel like she'd hurt him somehow? She was allowed to tell him when he'd overstepped. Communication was important. And he'd known that she didn't approve of lavish gifts. He could use his money however he wanted as long as he didn't use it excessively on her.

Izzie went from sitting on her couch to pacing the small living room to leaning against her fridge, to standing by her window. She hadn't seen Bart come or go from the casino. And their little conversations before bed each night didn't sway her opinion that something had shifted between them.

Okay, so maybe she'd been wrong. Was it possible she'd overreacted when he'd given her the guitar?

Correction: when he'd *attempted* to give her the guitar.

Izzie glanced over her shoulder toward the guitar stand that rested in the corner. It was strange the phantom itch her fingers had to play such an instrument. It had only taken a few minutes of handling the guitar to make her want to pluck the strings and hear the beautiful acoustic notes.

No. I've made the right decision.

If she didn't grow accustomed to money, she didn't have to feel the loss of it when it inevitably was ripped from her. Being frugal had been the only way she'd been able to survive after her father had taken everything from her.

A knock sounded at the door and she squealed as her heart jumped.

Izzie whirled around to stare at the door. It was nearly nine o'clock. Who would be visiting her at this hour? Olivia maybe?

The knock rapped at the door once more, jolting her into action. She swept across the room, hurrying toward the door. A peek through the spy hole had her sucking in a gasp.

Bart was standing outside her door. He shifted, looking down the hallway both ways then lifting his hand to knock for a third time.

Before his hand could make contact, she yanked the door open. He froze with his hand in the air and his eyes met hers. They stood like that, as if they were sizing each other up. Then he pulled his hand from behind his back to give her a single pink rose.

Her eyes landed on the pristine flower then bounced to his face.

He lifted a shoulder and gave her a crooked smile. "I missed you."

She let out a small laugh. "I missed you, too."

Bart nodded toward the apartment. "Can I come inside?"

Izzie moved to the side, nodding. "Of course."

He held out the flower, forcing her to accept it before he took a step inside. Bart hovered just inside the doorway, turning to face her when she shut the door.

"I'm sorry—"

"I wanted to—"

Both of them stilled then smiled.

Bart moved toward her, closing the distance between them. He slipped his hands around her waist and she melted against him when he pulled her closer. His voice was low and sent all sort of tingles and chills through her body. "I'm sorry. I should have asked before I bought you that guitar."

"That would have been a start." She tilted her head. "But I forgive you." She wrapped her arms around his neck. "But I should have been more patient with you. I need to remember to communicate a little better."

His brow lifted. "Does that mean you'll take the guitar?"

Her eyes widened and she let out a sharp laugh. "Of course not. You have to send it back, Bart. It's far too extravagant. I can't have it."

Bart's features grew slightly sullen. "Right."

She leaned up on her toes and brushed a feathery kiss to his lips. "But I'm glad you figured out a way to visit. I've been lonely without you." Her words breathed against his lips and then his cheek when she moved her attention across his face toward his ear. "I love you, Bart."

His hold on her tightened.

"You don't know how grateful I am for you. This last week has been so hard—not seeing you. Please tell me we don't have to do that again."

Bart pulled his head back enough that his eyes could be seen clearly. "I couldn't agree more."

Izzie grinned. "Are you going to stay awhile? Or do you have to be somewhere?"

He grasped her chin with his finger and thumb. "I don't have to be anywhere, but with you." His husky voice was almost too much to bear.

More chill rippled through her body and along every single nerve she had. Her focus dipped down to his mouth, recalling just how much she'd missed that part of him too.

Bart was far too detail oriented. He didn't miss the way she stared at him, nor the way she moistened her lips. He tilted her chin up and pressed a firm kiss against her lips. It was like he searched for something specific as his mouth roved over hers. She loved the way his kiss could claim every part of her. It was in the almost tentative way his kisses began but then he'd shift gears and make sure she knew he wanted her more than anything else.

He stepped into her, forcing her to move backward until she was pressed up against her door. His palm slammed against the door right above her shoulder as his kiss deepened. He'd missed her far more than she had anticipated and it only served to increase her own desire.

Their distance had starved her. It was like she'd wandered in the desert for the last week without food or water and his affection was the only thing that could quench her thirst. She clawed at his shirt, tugging him closer even though they were nearly chest-to-chest as it was.

Her breath grew ragged, and her legs weakened. If it wasn't for her hold on him, she would have surely crumpled to the floor before him. Dazed, she allowed herself to escape into the warmth of his embrace.

His kisses became less fervent and gentler until he withdrew from her. Only a few inches separated them, and his eyes seemed just as stunned over their sudden display of affection. Bart's chest lifted and dropped with short, sharp breaths but he still managed to force a laugh from his lips. "You don't know how much I've wanted to kiss you like that," he murmured.

Izzie's heart hammered erratically. It was he who had no idea how much he affected her. All she could do was smile and place her hand against his cheek. "I love you so much."

"I love you, too." Bart brushed a soft kiss against her lips, but she could feel him restraining the passion he'd just shown her. Bart chuckled as he pulled away. "I better go. If I don't, there's no telling what might happen next."

She shivered as his hands grasped her upper arms and he moved her to the side. Then he reached for the doorknob and glanced at her once more, a crooked grin on his face. "I love you, Izzie."

Her voice caught in her throat, but before she could respond, he continued.

"See you later?"

Izzie nodded. "See you later."

He opened the door and disappeared into the hallway.

She touched her fingers to her lips, moving to the door and then backing into it. Izzie rested her head against the wood and let out a small laugh. It was all her body could muster after what she'd just experienced. She pressed her lips together and bit down on them then laughed again. So this was what true love felt like.

As the next few weeks passed in a blur, it was almost like their relationship was brand new again. It was hard to believe they'd even had an argument. And now that she thought back to it, her stance on his gift *had* been somewhat harsh.

Every so often she thought back to her reaction and her face flushed. If she had gotten someone a thoughtful gift, she wouldn't want them to turn their nose up at it based on the cost—expensive or not. Yes, she had certain triggers. And avoiding those triggers would help with her mental state.

Bart was sweet enough to acknowledge them and since their little argument he'd made a wonderful effort to keep her preferences in mind. He was practically the perfect boyfriend and she wanted to do something for him that would show him how much she cared.

Izzie strode into Maple Gardens and headed straight for reception. Olivia's gaze remained on her computer screen as her chipper voice formed her rehearsed lines. "Welcome to Maple Gardens, how can I help—" Her eyes shifted toward Izzie and she brightened. "Izzie! I didn't think you were going to come visit your mom today."

Izzie flushed slightly. "I'll visit with her for a bit, but mostly I came to ask your advice."

Olivia stared at her blankly. "Oh? What did you need?"

Leaning over the counter, Izzie lowered her voice. "Can you take a break and we can go for a walk?"

Olivia's eyes rounded. "Is it serious?"

Shaking her head, Izzie straightened. "But I'd rather not discuss my personal life at the counter when other people would overhear." Her cheeks were still warm from the blush that had appeared a few moments before.

Olivia shot a quick glance at the clock. "You're in luck. My break is supposed to be in about ten minutes, but I can take it a little early." She turned to the other receptionist. "I'll be back in fifteen."

Together they headed down the hall that would lead them to the gardens. Olivia slipped her arm though Izzie's and lowered her voice almost conspiratorially. "So, what are we up to? What's so personal that you don't want complete strangers to find out?" She gasped and her grip on Izzie tightened. "Did Bart propose? Are you going to be a billionaire's wife?"

Izzie stiffened and her head whipped around to gape at her friend. "What? Absolutely not. I'm not going to marry the guy... and even if I was, we haven't been dating nearly long enough for something like that to even come up." Even as she said it, her heart fluttered and Bart's face filled her thoughts. There couldn't have been a more perfect guy for her to fall in love with. Wasn't that why she was here in the first place? She needed ideas.

"Well, what is it then?" Olivia's lower lip pouted. "Because I've heard some people fall in love and get married after only knowing each other a week."

"Yeah, and they're all divorced."

"Not true," Olivia argued. "Some of them have stayed together for the long haul because they found their soulmates and they knew it."

Izzie rolled her eyes. "I wouldn't say that Bart is my soulmate. I mean, think about it. We nearly broke up because he gave me the wrong gift."

Olivia pulled Izzie to a stop and gave her a pointed look. "And whose fault was that?"

Izzie squirmed. "I know. But if anyone would understand it would be you and Bart knew that I wasn't interested in expensive things. Besides—"

Her friend held up a hand. "You don't have to give me

any excuses. Yes, I know the disaster that was your child-hood. And you know my feelings on being gracious and accepting the gifts that people give. We can agree to disagree on that front. For all intents and purposes, Bartholomew is perfect. He's a family guy. He's handsome. He's generous. And to top it all off, he's *rich*."

Izzie shook her head, though a smile tugged at her lips. "Just because he's got all those things going for him, he's not perfect."

Olivia opened her mouth to argue, but Izzie stopped her with her own hand gesture.

"However, he is perfect for me." The smile she'd been holding back filled her face. "Which brings me to the reason why I'm here."

Olivia blinked, and for the first time, it appeared Izzie had made her friend speechless.

"I need your help coming up with something to get him. I want him to know how much I love him but what do you get a guy who can get anything he wants?"

A very unladylike bark of laughter exploded from Olivia's chest. "You're kidding, right?"

Brows creasing, Izzie glanced around where they now stood at the side of the courtyard. A few curious stares were tossed their way but she didn't recognize anyone and it wasn't like people could overhear who they were talking about. She turned back to Olivia. "What's so funny?"

She shook her head, amusement still filling her features. "I can't believe you don't see the irony here. You're asking for help in picking out a gift for Bart when you got so upset about the one he got you."

Izzie's mouth dropped open and she made a disgruntled noise. "This is different."

"Is it?"

"Of course it is. Whatever I get him isn't going to be some extreme, expensive object that is worth more than a house."

Olivia placed both of her hands on Izzie's shoulders and stared at her steadily. "But to Bart that wasn't a lot of money. It was like a drop in the bucket. You have to have perspective, Izzie."

She sniffed. "It's still not the same thing. I just want to find him something that will mean a lot to him but I have no idea what to get him."

Olivia sighed. "There's no changing your mind on this, is there?"

Izzie ignored her friend's statement. She had every right to choose how to react to such a gift. And neither Olivia nor Bart could boss her around about it.

"Fine, I'll help you. What does he like?"

"What do you mean?"

"Like... is he into sports? Does he like wine? What's he into?"

Izzie frowned. As much time as she'd spent with him, she didn't know nearly enough about him. "He works all day then spends time with me—usually at my place." In fact, she hadn't been to his place yet which was really strange. Was he hiding something? She shook off the twisty feeling in her stomach. Bart had been nothing but upfront about everything. She turned her focus back to Olivia. "He likes classic books. That's all I got."

Olivia arched a brow. "Well, my suggestion is to get to know him a little better before you decide what to get him. Then figure it out from there."

And the most reasonable way to do that would be to confront him and make him take her to his place.

Chapter Twenty

Bart twisted around in his office chair and rose to gaze out the window. If he'd been asked, he would have told anyone that his life was almost perfect.

Almost.

There was something missing, only he couldn't put his finger on it.

His relationship with Izzie had evened out and he loved spending time with her. It was funny the way things had shifted since he'd taken over Lawrence's business ventures. He'd moved to the city and into his uncle's penthouse suite. He'd taken over his uncle's offices. But then he'd met Izzie and now all his time was spent either working or at her place. They went on their fair share of dates. If it was a weekend, they could usually be found at a karaoke bar or at an estate sale. Otherwise, they usually curled up on the couch and watched a show or read a book.

For all intents and purposes, he had a wonderful life.

So why did he feel like something was just out of reach? It was like there was this itch in the recesses of his thoughts —like he was being held back by something.

Bart pushed the thought so far down back into his stomach where it wouldn't see the light of day. He wasn't about to borrow trouble right when things were starting to settle into a good place. Izzie was what he'd wanted. She was smart, and down to earth, and she had the voice of an angel. To him, she *was* an angel.

Behind him, his office door opened. Bart glanced over his shoulder to find his secretary poking her head inside. "Sir, there's an Izzie Davis here to see you."

His eyes widened and he spun around. "Are you certain?" Izzie hadn't stepped foot in his casino. She'd attempted that one time and had a panic attack. If she was willing to come into his office today, something must be wrong.

His secretary nodded but he was already charging across his office to open the door. Jillian stepped back quickly, revealing Izzie standing awkwardly by a window looking over the entrance of the casino below. Her head turned, eyes finding his.

She looked paler than usual, but other than that she appeared to be okay. Bart strode toward her. "Is everything okay? Did something happen with your mom? Are you—"

Izzie smiled and tucked a strand of hair behind her ear with a trembling hand. "I was visiting Maple Gardens this morning when I realized something." She glanced past him and he followed her focus to where Jillian shot them several curious glances. "Can we go into your office?"

He nodded and slipped her hand within his. "Of course." Her hand was cool to the touch, clammy. His heart beat a little faster and the vivid memory of their last argument came to the forefront of his mind. She wasn't here to break up with him, was she? He hadn't done anything wrong. The last time he left her, they were in a good place.

Was it possible she was feeling that same sense that something was off? Surely she would have told him.

Maybe that was why she was here today. She had felt it too, and she wanted to discuss a way to fix it.

He prayed he was right. Already he could feel his sense of confidence in their relationship unraveling. Izzie was the biggest bright spot in his life. He had even gone so far to fantasize what it would be like to stand before their family and friends and a priest to promise their lives to one another.

They escaped to the office and he shut the door quietly before turning to her. "Izzie, whatever it is—"

"Why haven't you invited me to your house... apartment... wherever you live?"

Bart blinked several times. She was right, they hadn't spent any time at his home.

She looked away and her cheeks filled with color. "I mean, I get it if you're not ready for our relationship to go that far. Or if you—"

He grasped both of her hands within his own. "There's no real reason I haven't taken you to my place. I..." He searched for the words. "I guess subconsciously, I figured you wouldn't want to go to my place because it used to be my uncle's."

Her eyes widened.

Bart gave her a sheepish grin. "You didn't like guys with money. You hate the place I work. In my defense, it just didn't seem like a place you would want to go."

She stared at him blankly and he couldn't tell if she was upset by his assumption of her or if he'd hit the nail on the head.

"On top of that," he glanced away and chuckled with embarrassment. "Before I moved here, I lived in a place much like yours. I find your apartment is a more comfortable place to be. My uncle's place doesn't quite feel like mine."

"But you've been living there for—"

His gaze swept back to meet hers. "I know. It's mine. I've moved in. But at the same time it still doesn't *feel* like mine. It's like I'm staying at my uncle's place and I can't invite guests over because..." Bart trailed off with another chuckle. "Why are you bringing this up anyway? Are you asking to visit?"

She nibbled on her lower lip and shifted her weight from one foot to the other. It looked like it took a great deal of effort to meet his eye line. "I suppose I am." She hurried on to add, "But only if you're ready for that sort of thing."

He tilted his head. "I think that sounds like a great idea."

A smile stole across her face, filling him with a mixture of relief and excitement. That niggling feeling that something was missing wasn't so strong. Had that been it? Had they needed a way to keep their relationship moving forward?

Bart hooked his finger under her chin and returned her smile. "I'd love to cook you dinner tonight, if you're not working."

Her eyes widened briefly. "You cook? Don't you have a housekeeper for that sort of thing?"

This time he laughed. "Izzie, I was a single guy who substituted at a high school. Do you think I could afford a housekeeper on that kind of salary?"

Izzie flushed again and attempted to look away but he kept ahold of her chin.

"I may not be much of a cook, but I know my way around a pot of pasta. How does fettuccini sound?"

"I think that sounds amazing. Is there anything I can bring?"

He moved his hand to her cheek, and traced his thumb over her cheekbone. "Absolutely not. Tonight is going to be all about you."

Something flickered in her countenance. It was brief, but he'd caught it. Something *was* still bothering her. Hopefully after tonight that would disappear completely.

Boy, he really shouldn't have bragged so much about cooking. He hadn't been lying about any of it, but he was severely out of practice and the proof was in sauce.

The fettuccini turned out...terrible. He didn't think he could mess up boiling water and putting pasta in it, but he was wrong. Some noodles stuck together, some were not quite cooked how he liked them and he even found a few that were overdone and practically disintegrating.

Bart stared at the mess of his kitchen in dismay. There was no fixing this before Izzie was to arrive and he'd let his housekeeper leave for the night. He'd been a fool to think he could cook after it had been so long. This most definitely wasn't like riding a bike.

The buzzer by the door sounded and he jumped. Izzie wasn't supposed to be here for another five minutes, but she was rarely late to anything. He put the strained noodles near the sink, wiped his hands on the apron he'd found in the pantry and hurried for the door. He yanked it open, the cool air from the hallway more refreshing than he'd like to admit. His face was flushed and all he wanted to do was request a raincheck.

Izzie stood in the hallway, holding a small cake. Her

eyes widened as they trailed over him and his unusual getup. One side of her mouth lifted with amusement. "Looks like you're having fun."

He rubbed the back of his neck and forced a feeble smile. "I may have overestimated my talents."

Her features faltered. She peered past him into his living room and it finally dawned on him. He hadn't completely welcomed her into his life. If the roles had been swapped, he might have assumed she was hiding something. Without a second thought, he pushed the door open wider. "Never mind. I can't promise that it's edible, but you can try it anyway."

She stepped past him, a look of relief and curiosity painted on her face. He'd made the right decision.

The apartment had an open floor concept. Everything was practically visible from the doorway beside his office and two bedrooms that were tucked into a hallway. He closed the door behind him and leaned into it until it clicked. Stepping up beside her, he gestured toward the apartment he hadn't even bothered to redecorate. There was the large sitting area with a leather sectional and an extravagant coffee table. A projector hung overhead, aimed at a large painting of a landscape scene. The screen was put away but could lower from the ceiling with a touch of a button.

There was a large dining area with a table that could seat at least eight people and then there was the kitchen where smoke had started escaping from the pot on the stove.

"My sauce..." Bart darted through the apartment toward the sauce. He lifted the lid and a splash of sauce bubbled out and hit the stovetop with a sizzle. He lunged for the pot's handle, forgetting to grab a hot pad and ended up burning his palm. "Ouch! Ow." He shook out his sore hand, grabbing the hot pad with his other hand and removing the pan from the stove.

"Here," Izzie's soft voice broke through the chaos and the burning pain in his palm. She had materialized beside him and had already taken his wrist, guiding him toward the sink. With a twist of her fingers, she had the faucet running.

He sucked in a sharp breath when she placed his hand under the coursing water. He glanced at her, meeting her eyes. "Thanks," he muttered. Could he have made more of a bad impression?

She offered him a small smile before she glanced around the mess of his kitchen. "Nice place."

His lips lifted into a wry smile. "It's usually in a much better state. Mrs. Hanley is going to kill me when she comes in tomorrow morning."

Izzie's brows furrowed. "Mrs. Hanley?"

"My housekeeper. Though sometimes she cooks for me, too."

Slowly, she nodded then her focus shifted around the rest of the apartment. "I think you could fit three of my apartments in here. What do you do with all of this space?"

He shrugged. "Oh, you know... host rave parties."

Her head snapped back around and she stared at him.

Bart chuckled. "Kidding." He nodded toward his hand. "I think it's going to be okay now."

She didn't move.

"You can let go of my wrist."

Izzie's eyes widened and she released him as quickly as he'd released the pan. "Sorry," she mumbled.

He snatched a hand towel and dried off his hand then quickly grasped her chin. "You have nothing to be sorry about." He pressed a soft kiss to her forehead then pulled back. "How about I give you the grand tour?" Bart glanced at the mess he'd made of dinner. "And then maybe we can order some pizza."

Izzie grinned. "I think that sounds perfect."

Chapter Twenty-One

It was strange being in *the* Bartholomew Brown's home. Yes, she was dating Bart, but being here in his place somehow made it feel different. The man who held Izzie's hand was not Bart anymore. He was the famous billionaire every girl in a five-hundred mile radius wanted to meet.

All of a sudden she was on edge. It was one thing to talk about his wealth when she couldn't see evidence of it.

Izzie swallowed down the anxiety that threatened to bubble up as Bart took her down the hall. The first room was his office. Two French doors with glass windows adorned the entrance. The room reminded her of that scene in that cartoon movie about the beast and that girl. The ceilings were high and on every wall but one, there were floor to ceiling shelves full of books.

Her eyes widened and she shot a shocked look in Bart's direction. He dropped her hand and motioned for her to go ahead and explore. In the center of the office was a desk that could probably be bigger than the bed she had in her apartment. She wandered by it, letting her fingers trail along the smooth, cool mahogany wood. She could imagine Bart in here, taking phone calls and doing his work.

What was more, she could almost imagine walking into this room and seeing him with his collar undone and his tie draped over his desk chair. There was a small reading nook near the large windows that lined one whole side of the room.

Chills raced through her body and she met Bart's eyes again before heading closer to the shelves. She let her hands drag along the edges of the solid wood shelves, feeling his eyes watching her. "Your uncle must have loved reading as much as you."

His warm chuckle wrapped around her like a hug. "Actually, this is the one room I had redesigned."

She paused and stared at him. "Really?"

Bart moved closer. "This room was his office. The desk was his. Even some of the furniture. But the walls were covered in art."

Izzie let her attention shift to the large bookshelves again. "What kind of art?"

He shrugged, finally closing the distance between them. His arms slipped around her waist and he pulled her against him. "My uncle was a fan of Van Gogh, mostly." He jerked his chin toward the wall to her right. "He had a replica of Starry Starry Night commissioned and it hung on that wall. There were several other works of art but that was the largest."

"What did you do with them?"

"I donated them."

Her mouth dropped open. "You didn't."

His lips quirked into a crooked smile. "I certainly did."

"Why would you do that?"

He glanced around the room. "Well, I prefer the

company of my books more than the art. Not to mention, they get to be admired by more people where they're at."

She let her gaze sweep through the room. Trying to imagine what it might be like in this room without all the shelves was nearly impossible. She pulled away from him and took a closer look at the titles on the shelves. "I think you might have too many books."

Bart smiled. "Never."

Izzie matched his grin. "You're probably right." Something strange caught her eye and she stopped. Her brows furrowed. "Why do you have so many copies of *To Kill a Mockingbird*?" It wasn't like the book was something special. None of his copies were special editions. They all looked like tattered versions that he might have used in his classrooms when teaching a unit on the time period.

Bart strode across the room and picked one off of the shelf she hovered near. He flipped open the cover and then turned it around to show her.

To my nephew. Hold your head up high no matter what.

She read the inscription then looked up at him. "Did your uncle write that?"

Bart shook his head then pulled out another copy, showing her another inscription similar to the last. Then another and another.

A smile played at her lips. "You must have every single copy of this book that has an inscription in it."

Once again, he should his head. "Not *every* copy." He placed the book on the shelf once more then leaned against it. "Uncle Lawrence did give me a copy and I lost it when I was a kid."

"You lost it?"

He rubbed the back of his neck with his hand and peered across the room. "Well, technically, I thought it was a dumb gift and I gave it to Goodwill. But now that he's at Maple Gardens and I'm here living in the place that was once his, I can't stop thinking about finding it and adding it to my collection."

"Are you telling me that you're looking for a book you gave away twenty years ago?"

Bart chuckled. "When you say it like that, you make me seem a little crazy."

"Oh, I don't think it's crazy," she said. "You're talking to the woman who walks into every pawn shop, attends every estate sale, and checks every auction for a necklace." Her eyes flitted to meet his. "I don't think it's crazy at all." Her eyes traced over every single copy he owned. There had to be at least two-dozen copies on the shelves. She reached for a copy and flipped it open. "What did your uncle write in yours?"

His focus shifted to the books and he gave her a sad smile. "Honestly, I don't remember. It's been too long. But I know I'll remember when I read it."

Izzie pushed the book back onto the shelf with the others. "It'll be really neat when you find it and you can add it to your collection."

"Yeah." His warm smile and the way his voice lowered to contain that husky tone gave her goosebumps.

Their eyes locked for what felt like a full minute. Bart seemed to lean in closer to her but it could be her imagination. He was already so close and the utter silence filled the air with tension. It was moments like this that reminded her that Bart was so much more than his money—and at the same time he was just a man like any other.

Then the view of the room in her peripheral came slamming against her and she forced herself to look away. It was still hard to be here in his home. She'd been so trained that money held this power over her and she was surrounded by things that reminded her how far different Bart was from her. Doubts crept into her soul. Their different outlooks on money was something deep down that she worried would divide them.

She needed to stop being so hard on him. Olivia's chastising words came back to her, dragging Izzie from descending into a pit of worry. Bart was a good guy. He'd done more than most men would. Hadn't he agreed to be more thoughtful regarding her view on money? That alone should give him bonus points.

Izzie pulled away from him, a bright smile on her face. "Are you going to finish the tour?"

He lunged forward and snatched her hand, tugging her closer. "Not yet."

Confusion swirled in her chest. "Was there something else you wanted to show me?"

Bart closed the distance, both pulling on her and stepping toward her. "You don't know how hard it has been to hold back with you, Izzie. From the moment I met you, I knew there was something special about you."

A flush crept up her neck, filling her face and she looked away. "There's nothing special about—"

He tipped her chin up, forcing her to meet his gaze. "Don't do that."

Her lashes fluttered. "Don't do what?"

"Give yourself some credit, Izzie." There was some bite to his voice. "You're an incredible woman and I know just how lucky I am to have you."

She blinked again.

"I have never seen someone work so hard to do the right thing in my entire life. And now that I run in somewhat different social circles, it's even more apparent. It is like people have stopped caring. People only do the right thing when others are watching. But those values go out the door the second they feel comfortable. But not with you."

"You don't know that."

"Oh I know a lot more than you think I do. I'm observant, Izzie. I've always had to be. And if I know one thing, it's that you are the most generous, kind, caring person. You sacrifice so that others don't have to. I can't even imagine what you would do if you were to win the lottery."

Her chest tightened and she willed herself to relax. He wasn't talking about money. It was just an example. This was about her. It was hard to rewire the way she viewed things when she was around him. She swallowed hard and shoved down her deep-seated anxieties, focusing on his words.

"If there is one thing I've realized since meeting you, it's that I want you in my life for the long haul."

Her eyes widened and she attempted to pull away. This was sounding more and more like a proposal.

Bart chuckled, his grasp on her tightening. "Don't worry. I know you're not ready to make any of this permanent. I just want you to know my intentions. Whatever happens, Isobel Davis, I intend on having you in my life indefinitely." He finally relaxed his hold on her but this time she didn't move away from him. Bart was something else. He was so down to earth and so flexible. He genuinely cared about her and how she felt. How could she not want what he offered?

Izzie gave him a hesitant smile. This was it, the turning point in their relationship where she decided if she was on the same path as Bart. Shoving aside all misgivings and worries, she nodded. "I think that sounds wonderful."

It wasn't a lie. Not really. If she could get past her

misgivings, she knew that being with Bart could be a grand adventure. The only thing she couldn't control were the outside forces that very well could be inevitable.

Bart showed her the rest of his apartment, from the oversized master suite to the spare room that held even more books. She hadn't known what to expect, but his place wasn't it. While there were clear extravagances in every room, most of what made this place his were the simple things and she had to remind herself that he'd inherited most of what she saw.

The best part of visiting Bart's place was that she had grown a little more comfortable being with him. He was so transparent. Even as he took her hand and led her toward the main living space, she had to admit she'd managed to win the lottery with him. He moved into the kitchen, releasing her hand as he picked up a phone.

Bart ordered pizza from the restaurant on the ground floor of his building then headed toward the couch. He sat down and patted the cushion beside him with a grin. She remained leaning against the counter in the kitchen, giving him a shy smile. She gnawed on her lower lip and let out a shaky breath. Pushing away from the counter, she moved toward him.

Before she could settle onto the cushion beside him, he grasped her hips and sat her square on his lap. His soft fingers brushed her hair behind her ear. "I hope I didn't freak you out back there."

Goosebumps lifted on her arms as she leaned into his touch. "I'd be lying if I said I wasn't surprised." She swallowed back the worry that always came with making this sort of move. "But it's the next step. I can see that."

He smiled and that pleasant, unsteady feeling increased.

"I can't believe I found a guy who is as patient and understanding as you." His fingers continued to graze her skin, causing her breath to hitch in her chest. "We come from two totally different worlds and yet I feel like we can make it work."

"I feel the same." His husky voice made her whole body melt. Who was she fooling? She wanted to be with him more than she wanted anything else in the world. She had just been too stubborn to see it.

Izzie leaned down, digging her fingers into his hair and capturing his mouth with hers. Electricity sparked between them, urging her forward. If she married him, this would be her life. She would never have to worry about money or how she was going to pay for the next bill. But they could still live fugally. It was the perfect combination.

His hands tightened on her hips and he pulled her close, forcing her to wrap her arms around his neck as they deepened their kiss.

While she still disliked the idea of his wealth, he'd proven that he was willing to abide by the rules she'd laid out. What could possibly go wrong?

Chapter Twenty-Two

Bart took a bite of his slice of pizza and grinned at Izzie. She sat beside him on the couch, her legs over his lap and eating her own piece. She beamed back at him. The good place that he'd wanted to get, that was here in this moment.

If he were to die right now in this moment he'd die happy. Pizza, the company of a wonderful woman, and the possibility of so much more.

He put his crust on his plate and brushed the crumbs from his fingers. "I have a feeling we're going to have to make this a tradition."

She tilted her head and swallowed. "I think I'd like that very much." Izzie lowered her legs to the floor. She put her plate on the coffee table and reached for a glass of water but her hand froze mid-air.

His gaze shifted to a newspaper she stared at.

Izzie grabbed the paper with shaking hands.

"Is everything okay?"

Her wide, green eyes bounced to meet his and she shoved the paper into his chest. "Look."

His mouth lifted on one side. "Easy." Bart accepted the

paper and glanced down at the headline and read it out loud. "Rare jade necklace to be auctioned at charity gala." Bart lifted his eyes to meet hers. "Do you think it's the right one?"

She hopped closer to him, settling beside him. She yanked the newspaper from him and flipped it over before punching her finger at the picture. "It's the right one." Her voice was hoarse, bordering on distraught.

"Are you okay? Isn't this a good thing? You found it."

Izzie slumped against the cushions. "You read it. The headline says rare. How on earth am I going to be able to beat out a bunch of rich people? I only have four grand. I guarantee it's going to go for more than that."

"You don't know that." His brows furrowed. Maybe he didn't understand. "Izzie, I can help you—"

She shot up in her seat. "No. I'm not going to let you do that."

"Izzie." Even he hated the patronizing way he said her name but he continued anyway. "I love you. I'm not going to let this slip between your fingers."

She shook her head vehemently. "I can't expect you to just come to my rescue anytime money is involved."

"Why not? I'm your boyfriend, Izzie and I would love to help you reclaim this."

Izzie glowered at him. "I'm not going to take advantage of you. I refuse to be the stereotypical girl who marries a billionaire for his money."

He scoffed. "We both know that couldn't be further from the truth." Bart forced his voice to soften. "Izzie, this means a lot to you. As such, it means a lot to me. Let me help you." Every part of her body was stiff. From the scowl on her face to the way she sat on the couch. He reached for her hand and brought it to his lips. "Please," he murmured.

Her eyes darted away and she rose, pulling her hand from his. She was going to let him help. He could feel it in his bones. He'd worn her down. Or maybe the necklace was more important than her ego.

Bart stood, leaving the newspaper on the couch.

Finally Izzie turned toward him. "You can help."

A smile broke across his face and he took a step toward her.

Izzie held up a hand, stopping him in his tracks. "But only by matching what I have. I won't have you throwing away your money on this."

"Izzie—"

"I mean it, Bart. If we can't get it for eight thousand, then we're not going to get it."

His focus shifted to the newspaper. Izzie had been right about one thing. With a headline like that, there was no way they'd get their hands on that necklace, not without dropping a lot more money. If he wanted to guarantee that the necklace returned to its rightful owner, he'd have to make a hard decision.

Bart glanced back at Izzie, finding her stern, expectant expression on him. "Whatever you want."

Her whole body relaxed and she practically threw herself against him—something she wouldn't have done if she knew what he was thinking. He'd have to take a calculated risk. They'd grown so close. She couldn't possibly hate him forever as long as she got the necklace, could she?

They'd both grown in this relationship. There had to be concessions made.

Bart couldn't remember the last time his hands were this clammy. He'd wiped them on his handkerchief at least half a dozen times from the moment he'd picked up Izzie from her place to the moment they arrived at the large building in front of them. A horde of paparazzi hovered just outside the high-rise building when his limo pulled up to the front doors.

This auction had drawn national attention but not just because the necklace was highlighted. There were several works of art listed on the directory along with other highly expensive items.

He'd made several calls regarding this event. First, he'd tried to buy the necklace, hoping they'd just remove it from the listing. But they refused. That was when he contacted those he knew who might be interested in the necklace and called in some favors. Everyone he spoke with agreed not to bid.

He only had one other trick up his sleeve and he hoped it wouldn't be necessary.

"Ready?"

Izzie's nervous voice yanked him from his thoughts and he glanced up at her. He nodded just as the driver opened their door.

Flashes of light blinded him when he emerged from the vehicle. Bart straightened his jacket and reached for Izzie's hand. Her porcelain skin practically glowed as she held on tightly and climbed out of the limo.

The flashes seemed to explode. While they'd been seen together, this was the first public event they'd been to as a couple. Izzie offered him a weak smile, but all he could see was her beauty.

She wore a deep green dress his secretary had managed to borrow from a New York designer. The color made her eyes pop. The silk fabric hugged every curve of her body, exemplifying her beauty.

Bart slipped her hand into the crook of his arm and they moved down the carpet toward the building. Photographers called out to them. Izzie's grasp on him tightened and he offered smiles to the spectators. This was the life he was dragging Izzie into. It wasn't any wonder that she didn't feel comfortable, but the way she handled it right now proved she was up for the challenge.

Once inside, the noise died down immediately. Izzie let out a heavy breath and a strangled laugh. "That's insane. I can hear my heartbeat in my ears. I was probably an absolute mess out there." Her hands pressed against her cheeks. "Do you think they noticed?"

He grasped her chin and tilted it up. "You were beautiful."

She smiled and her cheeks filled with color. "Thank you," she murmured.

Bart placed his hand on the small of her back. The gown dipped so low that his skin was able to touch hers. She shivered, the electricity that flowed between them still strong.

They retrieved their signs and moved through the crowd of people, dodging groups who were chatting about what was up for auction. They arrived in the room where the auction would be held and his gaze swept along every square inch of it until they landed on Isaac.

His friend sat near the side, already seated. He turned, as if he could feel Bart's gaze on him then he nodded. Bart nodded back.

"Who's that?"

Bart jumped peering down at Izzie. "Hmm?"

"The guy you were looking at."

He glanced back to where Isaac was now faced forward. "An old friend."

"Oh."

Bart guided her toward the front and they took their seats near the aisle. Their position would allow them to get a good look at the necklace just in case she was wrong. Slowly the room filled, the excited chatter growing louder.

Izzie was jitterier than he could remember her being so he rested his hand on her knee. She stilled, shooting him an appreciative look.

He leaned toward her. "Don't worry. We'll get it."

"I hope so."

He did too.

Soon the auction was underway. Each item was brought before the crowd and with each one, the tension in his shoulders increased. Guests held up their signs as the auctioneer prattled off their bids.

"The next item is a jewel of grand proportions," the auctioneer quipped. "Our appraisers have confirmed the quality and size of the jade stone and you can find that information in your pamphlets..."

Izzie's hand reached out and snatched his, tightening around his fingers with such force he grimaced.

"We'll start the bidding at one thousand."

She sucked in a sharp breath.

If he had to guess, he would have assumed her reaction was due to how high the starting bid was. The stone in his stomach agreed with her sentiment.

Bart glanced over his shoulder, finding Isaac's eyes on him once more before he turned his attention to the auctioneer.

"Do I have two-thousand and five hundred?" Izzie lifted her card and the bidding war commenced.

His heart raced, his hand hurt, and the bids were going far too fast for comfort. By the time they hit seven thousand, there were still five bidders in the game. There was no way they'd win. The rock in his stomach grew even heavier.

"Eight thousand and five hundred!" The auctioneer pointed out in the crowd somewhere.

Bart dragged his focus to Izzie. The blood had drained from her face. It wasn't too late. She could still win if she would just put aside her silly notions about money. "Izzie, let me—"

"No," she bit out. "You agreed." A tear slipped down her cheek and she brushed at it with the back of her hand. "I know you don't understand," her voice shook, "but it is very important I do this my way." She rose from her seat and moved past him, her skirt clenched in her hand as she hurried down the aisle toward the door. He twisted in his chair, his eyes following her. Several other guests did the same.

He settled back in his chair, heart heavy. The bids had slowed down. They were now at twelve-thousand dollars. The worst part was that he knew he could afford it. This wasn't about the money for him. It was about a legacy—something that mattered to *her*. It was like the book he continued to look for. Who cared if it was expensive? He had the means to make this right, and dang it, he was going to do it.

Bart twisted once more in his chair, finding Isaac's face in the sea of people. He gave his friend a sharp nod and rose from his chair to follow Izzie from the room.

Isaac lifted his card and the auctioneer shouted, "Thirteen thousand to bidder number forty-seven. Do I hear thirteen thousand and five hundred?"

Bart strode down the aisle and out of the large ballroom. In the lobby area, Izzie was nowhere to be found. She'd vanished. He quickened his steps. She had to still be here somewhere. She could be in the bathroom. Or she might have gone outside to get some air.

He'd find her and help her through this. Then he'd have to come up with a way to break it to her that he'd gone against her rules. But that could be another time. Her emotions were too volatile at the moment. He didn't want to set himself up for failure. She'd gotten pretty mad at him over the guitar. There was no telling how she'd react to the necklace.

Bart glanced toward the hallway where the bathrooms would be located, but his gut told him not to bother. He'd like to think he knew Izzie well enough that he could count on her going outside, so that's where he went.

Right as he got through the doors, his eyes landed on Izzie down the cement steps hailing a taxi. His heart launched into his throat and he charged down the steps. "Izzie! What are you doing?"

She shot an apologetic look in his direction as she opened the door to the cab. Bart all but tumbled down the last few steps and reached her just in time to stop the door from shutting. Oxygen ripped through his chest, making his lungs ache. "Izzie," he wheezed, "where are you going?"

"Home." She scowled, refusing to meet his gaze.

"I can take you home."

This time she lifted her bright green eyes toward him. "No."

"No? You can't be serious."

She let out a sigh and a tear slipped down her cheek. "I've been hunting for that necklace for the better part of... I've lost count of how many years. Let me go home and grieve the thing that I will never have a chance at getting."

"You know that's not true." It took everything in his power to keep his voice even and not to yell at her. "I told you I could—"

"Lady, am I taking you home or not? The meter's running."

Bart ducked down to glower at the man. "Can you wait a minute?"

"Just call me tomorrow, Bart. I'll be fine. Just let me mourn what I've lost. Okay?" She pleaded with him, her voice a breath above a whisper.

He should tell her—drag her out of this disgusting cab and tell her that she was being ridiculous and he had taken matters into his own hands. But he knew better. This conversation would be better if he treaded carefully.

Bart stepped back and shut the door. The taxi pulled away from the curb and into traffic. He clenched and unclenched his hands. She'd have to get used to him doing little favors for her. What good was a billion dollars if he couldn't use it to help the people he loved? She'd forgive him. She'd be crazy not to.

Chapter Twenty-Three

The weight of the world had officially fallen on her shoulders. Each breath Izzie took was racked with a deep ache she couldn't shrug off this time. The necklace had been so close, she could have sworn she felt the heavy gold chain in her fingers.

She stared down at her empty hands and a sucked in a shuddering breath. If she didn't get home soon, she'd be bawling in the back of this taxi car. Already the driver had shot her a few concerned looks.

Whoever bought the necklace would definitely keep it. She hadn't even realized it was a rare stone. This new knowledge only filled her with more fury—at her father, at her mother, and at herself.

If her father hadn't given it away... if her mother had been shrewd enough to keep it hidden... if she'd found it sooner.

There were plenty of people who would say she was overreacting. It was a piece of jewelry, for heaven's sake. Maybe it was time to let that piece of her family disappear and never look back. Izzie was starting a new life with new relationships. Her father was out of the picture. She was healing. And her mother was finally in a good place.

But how do I tell her?

Izzie leaned against the door arm rest and stared outside at the buildings and landscape that they passed by. She felt hollow, without purpose and all she wanted to do was go home. She'd slip out of her dress, climb into bed, and cry herself to sleep.

In the morning she'd figure out how to break it to her mother that she wasn't able to get the necklace.

The cab pulled up to her building. She mumbled her thanks and climbed out of the car, her heels dangling from her fingers. Barefoot, and desolate, she climbed the steps to her apartment, not seeing anything but blurry figures. Tears filled her eyes and tumbled down her cheeks, making it hard to focus.

Her fingers fumbled with the keys until she at last got the door open. The keys were tossed on the table near the door and she managed to get out of her dress to climb into bed. Sleep came, black and unforgiving.

Incessant pounding. Someone calling her name. Izzie was in a foggy clearing. She couldn't see more than a few feet in front of her.

"Isobel Davis."

More pounding.

"Are you home? This is the courier. They should have told you I was coming."

Confusion swirled with her foggy surroundings.

The doorbell rang, dragging her from her sleep.

Izzie winced against the bright light coming into her

room. She covered her hand over her eyes and blinked a few times. The bell buzzed once more.

She gasped and launched from her bed, grabbing her robe. But she only got a few steps. The blood drained from her head too fast and she had to grip the door jamb to prevent herself from collapsing on the floor. It almost felt like she had a hangover.

Well, that's exactly what she had. She'd cried herself to sleep and the residual consequences were now plaguing her. She squeezed her eyes shut and called out, "Coming. One minute."

Once her apartment came into focus, she moved with more caution toward the front door. Her hand tightened around the knob and she pulled the door open. Her brows were creased as she took in the young man in front of her.

He had dark hair and a bare amount of stubble. He wore a suit and he carried a small box in his hands. Behind him was a security officer who didn't look too pleased to be there in her hallway. She squinted at them, pulling her robe around her a little tighter. "How can I help you?"

"Isobel Davis?"

She nodded. "That's me."

"My name is Gerald and I'm from the auction last night."

Izzie shook her head. "I'm sorry. You're from the auction?"

He nodded. "I'm going to need to see some identification before I can give you what you won."

"I'm sorry," she repeated, "but I didn't win anything."

Gerald glanced back at the officer and held out his hand. The officer handed him a small notebook which Gerald flipped through. "Item forty-two, a jade necklace—"

"What? No. I didn't..." Her whole body went hot and

cold all at once. Every nerve ending hummed with angry electricity. "Bart," she growled.

"Pardon?"

Izzie shook her head sharply. "That's not my necklace."

Confusion filled Gerald's face and he pointed to the notebook. "Your name is right here—"

"I don't care what it says. I didn't win that necklace."

"My apologies, ma'am. But I've been sent out here to deliver this piece of jewelry to you. It has been paid for—"

"I'm sure it has." She folded her arms and leaned against the door jamb. "Just take it back. Or take it to Bartholomew Brown."

The poor guy looked absolutely flabbergasted. He exchanged a look with the officer. "I can't do that. Your name is on the release form. We can call the curator and try to get this sorted—"

Izzie groaned and moved inside, leaving the two men in the hall. It wasn't their fault she had wrongfully trusted her boyfriend to respect her wishes. But she knew how to fix this. She snatched her purse and returned to the doorway, holding out her driver's license.

Gerald handed the notebook to the security officer and retrieved his phone. He took a quick picture of the identification then held out the small box toward her. "Congratulations on your win—"

The death-glare she gave him was probably enough to turn him to stone. She snatched the box from his hand and he jumped. Without another word, she slammed the door shut.

It only took her five minutes to pull on a sweatshirt and a pair of jeans. She didn't bother fixing her hair but when she glanced in the mirror she knew she'd have to clean the streaked makeup before leaving the apartment.

Those poor men.

They didn't deserve my rudeness.

She brusquely wiped under her eyes and down her cheeks where the mascara had streaked then tossed the rag in the sink. Bart was going to get a piece of her mind, and a new piece of jewelry.

Izzie didn't heed Bart's secretary as she stormed toward Bart's office. She didn't even know if he was here. But based on the way his secretary was acting, she'd lucked out. Izzie charged through the door, letting it bang open.

Bart glanced up from where he sat at his desk. He jumped up from his seat. "Hey there, how are you feeling?"

She tossed the box at his chest and it bounced onto his desk. "What. Is. That?"

His eyes followed the jewelry box and then lifted to meet her angry gaze. "Oh."

Izzie muttered a bad word beneath her breath. "Yeah. *Oh.*"

Bart picked up the necklace. "They weren't supposed to deliver it for a few days at least. I thought I had more time to—"

"More time to what?" She seethed. "To convince me that I was wrong? To make me come around to you swooping in here like some knight in shining armor and fix this?" Her breaths came out hot and heavy. "Well, guess what? I'm no damsel in distress and you are most certainly not my knight."

He held the jewelry box in his hand, then moved it to the other and back. "I'm not sorry."

She threw up her hands. "Of course you're not. You

think you can do whatever you want without any regard for my feelings."

His features scrunched into a glower and he put the box on his desk. "No. You don't get to decide what I do with *my* money. You don't have a say in how I want to help those I *love*." His voice caught on that last word and he took a step toward her. "That necklace means the world to you," he whispered huskily. He jabbed a finger toward it. "I knew that it was more important than anything."

"More important than us?" she hissed.

His whole body stiffened. "What?"

"You heard me. Is that necklace more important than our relationship? Because that's what you seem to be telling me since you decided to go behind my back and buy the dang thing." Her heart hammered and her blood roared in her ears. It was like she'd somehow become separate to herself. Somewhere overhead she was floating, watching as she sabotaged the only good thing she had going for her.

"You can't be serious."

"Oh, I'm deadly serious. I'm not keeping that necklace, Bart. I couldn't afford it so it doesn't belong to me."

"Do you even hear yourself?" He raked both his hands through his hair. "What do you want me to do? I can't take it back."

"Why not?"

He let out a sharp laugh. "Because it's paid for."

"Then donate it."

Bart's animated features smoothed into something almost scarier than his anger. He picked up the necklace and closed the distance between them. His voice lowered to a whisper and he reached for her hand. He placed the box in one hand then grasped the other as if trying to assure her. "I love you but you are not thinking clearly. You'll take the necklace and you'll appreciate it when everything has finally settled."

She tore her hand out of his grasp, the laugh that ripped from her throat didn't sound like her own. "I will not let you control me. Either you take it back, or we're through." She held the necklace out to him.

He blinked.

Izzie was just as surprised by her ultimatum, but once the words had slipped from her lips, there was no taking them back. This whole thing had gotten wildly out of hand. She didn't want to break up with him but she couldn't just let him walk all over her. She'd drawn a line in the sand and she expected him to listen.

Money was a touchy subject. And it would always be.

He folded his arms, his chin lifting. "So be it."

Her eyes widened. "Are you serious?"

"Are you?" he snapped.

They stared each other down for what felt like ages but was probably only a few seconds. Teeth clenched, she glared at him. "Fine." Izzie's fingers tightened around the jewelry box and her hand dropped to her side. She spun on her heel, ready to charge the door behind her.

Bart's hand shot out and grabbed her forearm.

Her head whipped around. His grip couldn't be construed as hard. It was gentle but unyielding, as he made her face him head on. Slowly, she lifted her gaze to meet his. "Let. Go."

He shook his head. "Please don't."

"You're the one who made this happen, Bart." She couldn't bear to keep her focus on his heartbroken expression, mostly because she could relate. The emotion and tremors that started in her gut had moved up into her chest and were now forcing themselves out. Her jaw trembled and her eyes brimmed with moisture. "I can't be with someone who won't listen to me and support my decisions," she rasped. "I can't be with you."

His hold on her tightened slightly. "Izzie..."

She shook her head as the fight left her body. "I'm sorry, Bart. I just can't. Please... just let me go."

Bart released her arm as if it had caught on fire. He took a quick step backward and she spun around before the first tear could slip down her cheek.

In half a dozen steps, she was out of his office. Her feet couldn't carry her fast enough. By the time she made it outside, her cheeks were completely covered with angry, salty remnants of her broken heart.

This was not how the conversation was supposed to go. She hadn't planned on breaking up with him, but it made sense. Deep down, she knew that Bart would never change. He would always view her as someone he needed to save.

She'd decided long ago that she would never rely on another person for anything.

Not even a billionaire like Bartholomew Brown.

Chapter Twenty-Four

"Ouch," Isaac chuckled. "Maybe I don't want to find what you have."

Bart glowered at his friend. "Did we schedule this meeting to chitchat or to finalize the donations I have coming to you?"

Isaac's amusement didn't leave his face. "Are you sure you don't want to talk about it? I can be a good listener." His teasing tone only fueled Bart's fury.

"I don't have time for this." He shot out of his seat but Isaac's chuckle stopped him.

"Settle down, Bart. We both know she will reconsider. It was a necklace for goodness sake. It's not like you cheated. I don't know of any girl who would be crazy enough to break up over a gift."

Well, he didn't know Izzie as well as Bart did. Bart swallowed hard and forced his clenched hands to relax. He returned to his seat at the conference table. The large room felt so big especially since his uncle wasn't in it.

Bart pushed the folder that had remained at his place toward Isaac. "These are my preferences."

Isaac reached for the folder, flipped it open then leaned back in his chair. His focus flicked over the documents in his hands until his relaxed, smooth features faltered. His eyes cut to meet Bart's over the top of the folder and he slowly placed the folder on the table. "Are you certain you want to do this? Considering the current circumstances?"

Bart folded his arms, his eyes not leaving Isaac's. "This document was drawn up a few days ago. What happened two nights ago has nothing to do with my decision."

"It's a little... spiteful, don't you think? Considering her reasons for breaking up with you."

"Spiteful?" His mouth formed the word in a sneer. "Izzie's mother deserves to be taken care of even if Izzie can't do it on her own. And no, this decision wasn't made because I'm in love with Margaret's daughter. It was made because Margaret is the only thing that seems to bring joy to my uncle right now. If Margaret couldn't afford to continue living at Maple Gardens, where does that leave Uncle Lawrence?"

Hesitant understanding filled Isaac's face. He tapped his fingers on the solid wood table, as if contemplating the repercussions that might occur with this sort of announcement.

"My only request is that you don't tell Izzie where the money is coming from."

Isaac's brows shot up. "How can you ask me to do that? You realize that she's not going to accept anything but the truth, right? Based on what you told me about her—"

"Tell her that there was a lottery drawing for the residents. Tell her that Lawrence had a surplus and it was decided that it went to those who make him happy. Tell her that there was a mistake in accounting for all I care. Just don't tell her that I'm the one who authorized it." He pushed his chair out from the table. "I have more meetings to get to." That was a lie, but he was tired of talking about Izzie. Every time he said her name, another piece of his heart shattered.

"Bart?"

He stopped as he got to the door, his hand resting against the handle, but he didn't turn toward his friend.

"You're a good man."

Bart nodded, but if he were to speak, his voice would crack and the emotion he'd been holding at bay would break the dam. He pushed the door open and headed down the hall.

He hadn't visited his uncle since his fight with Izzie, mostly because he didn't know what he would do if he saw her. Part of him knew he wouldn't have much control over himself. He'd go back on everything he said. He might even tell her that he was wrong when deep down he knew he wasn't. He needed to stay strong, firm in his decision.

He let out a shaky breath as he made it to the elevator. The doors opened and a pretty woman smiled at him as he got inside.

They stood side by side as they descended toward the lobby. She twirled a strand of hair in her fingers and glanced at him. "You're Bartholomew Brown, aren't you?"

Bart glanced at her out of the corner of his eye. "Yeah."

"I read an article about you the other day. Your charitable donations are so generous. Your uncle couldn't have picked a better man to take over."

"Thanks," he muttered thickly.

She dug around in her purse. Thank goodness. While he knew he was doing good, and he wanted to help people who couldn't help themselves, he didn't like the spotlight nearly as much as his uncle did. That's not why he did the good he was known for.

The woman finished with whatever she was doing when the elevator doors opened. He took a step toward the door and her hand reached out to stop him. He glanced down at what she held out to him—a small slip of folded paper. "My name is Bella. Call me." She blushed and hurried out of the elevator before he could tell her he was involved.

Except he wasn't. Izzie had broken up with him.

Bart looked at the slip of paper. It almost felt wrong to be holding it, to be considering what it might be like to forget all his problems by taking a pretty girl out. Bella probably wouldn't get mad at him over buying her gifts.

His hand wrapped around the piece of paper, crumpling it in his fist. No. He might be weak right now. He might not know where his future with Izzie might go, but he could have hope. He could bide his time, wait her out. And if she never forgave him, at least he would be able to say that he didn't have any regrets. Bart tossed the phone number into the garbage can right outside of the elevator and strode toward the doors.

"You *what*? Izzie! You can't do that."

Izzie glanced at Olivia out of the corner of her eye, irritation filling her body to the brim. "You sound just like him."

"Because he's right." Olivia stared at the necklace in her hands. "If this is as valuable as you say it is, there is no way you would have ever been able to afford it. Bart basically gave you the moon, and you slapped his face. Or might as well have."

Izzie flinched. It had only been three days since their fight and she hadn't gotten any sleep. Several times she'd been tempted to call him, visit him. She couldn't deny that she felt guilty over her reaction. She didn't even say thank you.

Her face burned and she turned away from her friend before Olivia could see the blush. If Olivia even sensed the remorse Izzie felt over the whole debacle, then she'd be pushing Izzie out the door before Izzie could explain herself.

Olivia closed the box and set it on the counter. "So what are you going to do with it?"

Izzie picked up a dirty dish from the sink and scrubbed it in the soapy water. "What do you mean?"

"Are you going to give it to your mom? Are you going to donate it like you told him to?"

Izzie knew she was going to regret telling Olivia everything about their conversation. Olivia had a way of shining a light on situations like these that made Izzie feel even worse. Already she was itching to call Bart right now and ask to see him.

Her hand tightened on the scrubber and she brushed furiously at the plate in her hand. "That's a stupid question."

"Izzie!" Shock laced Olivia's voice.

Izzie cringed, her shoulders drooping. "Sorry," she muttered. "Of course I'm going to give it to my mother. It belongs to her."

"You want to know what I think?"

"Not really," she murmured. "But I have a feeling you're going to tell me anyway."

"Darn straight I am." Olivia moved toward her. She picked up a clean dish and a hand towel then started drying the dishes Izzie had finished washing. "I think your heart is broken."

"That's not a surprise. Bart broke my heart when he went against my wishes."

Olivia shook her head. "Nope. Bart is trying to help you heal."

Izzie froze, her hands hovering over the sink as she gaped at Olivia.

"Hear me out. Your father broke your heart when he did your family wrong."

Chills crawled down Izzie's spine. Her whole body flashed cold then hot, as if acknowledging what Olivia had seemed to figure out without even trying.

"When your dad broke your heart, you taped it up, fixed it however a little girl could, then locked it away in an iron box and hid the key." Olivia gave her a pointed look. "You refuse to let any guy take care of you. I don't think I have ever seen you open up to a guy—not even to Bart. Well, okay, Bart has seemed to get the closest."

A lump, heavy, hard and unforgiving formed in Izzie's throat. As much as she wanted to shout, yell, and tell Olivia that she needed to shut up and drop the issue, a small part of her wanted—needed—her to keep going.

Olivia picked up another dish and continued working. "You've been scared of being hurt like your dad hurt you and your mom and you've gotten so used to keeping every-thing locked away. But then along comes Bart, a smart, kind, generous billionaire—and you are scrambling. He's figured out how to get past your defenses but now he's standing at the final gates and all he wants is for you to let him in. He wants to take care of you Izzie. That's all."

Izzie's brows lowered but only to hide the pain that was probably etched on her face. "I don't need anyone to take care of me."

Olivia snorted. "Everyone needs someone to take care of them. We're not solitary creatures."

She made several good points. And as much as Izzie hated it, she knew that she'd have to do something soon if she wanted to fix the mess she'd made.

Her sense of betrayal over what he'd done wasn't logical even as she clung to every last thread of her reasoning. A sob caught in her throat and she put the cup in her hand into the water. Her shoulders slumped and she held herself around the waist as the tears flowed. She wasn't crying over Bart, not really. She was crying over the childhood, the trust, the optimism that her father had stolen from her.

Bart had been the only one who was strong and persistent enough to be what she needed to heal.

Olivia's arm draped around her shoulders and she pulled her close. Izzie cried into her friend's shoulder until the sobs that racked her body settled. When they stopped, the only sound in her apartment was that of her sniffles. Olivia's hands trailed up and down Izzie's back. She continued to be the voice of reason when Izzie needed her most.

"I don't know what I would do without you."

"I know." There was a smile in the way she'd said it. So Olivia.

They pulled apart and Izzie let out a watery laugh. "So what do I do now? I can't just go knock on his door and tell him I was wrong."

"Why not? He's a guy. Men live for the times when women tell them they were right all along."

They both laughed. "Seriously, though. I need to do something."

Olivia frowned. "I have no idea. You said he was looking for that book, maybe you could try finding it?"

Izzie shook her head and they headed over to the couch, the dishes forgotten. "He's been looking for that book for years. There's no way I would be able to find it."

Olivia pressed her lips together and reached for a newspaper from the coffee table. "I guess we'll have to brainstorm. Maybe you could write a song?"

Izzie's blush returned. She gestured around the room. "I didn't let him give me the guitar either, remember?"

The situation was so sad it was almost funny. Olivia flipped a page. "Yeah, you really bit yourself in the behind with this one, didn't you?"

"You're not being very helpful, you know that right?"

Olivia flashed her a smile. "If I was good at this whole relationship thing, I'd be married to my own billionaire by now." Her eyes dipped to the newspaper. "Bart donated a bunch of art to a gallery, right?"

"Yeah."

"Maybe you take him to a gallery. He probably likes the artsy scene." She flipped open the newspaper to show a page filled with images of young artists. The title read, 'High School Students Art Showcase One Weekend Only'.

Izzie snatched the newspaper from Olivia, garnering a disgruntled sound. Her eyes scanned the article. "I don't believe it," she murmured.

Olivia scooted close to her and peered over the side. "What?"

"These are high school students."

"Yeah..." she drawled. "So what?"

"Bart used to be a substitute teacher at this school!"

Olivia's eyes widened. "He was a *high school* teacher? Geez, Izzie. You hit the jackpot with this guy! Why did you break up with him again?"

Izzie shot her friend a dark look then returned her focus to the article. "This is amazing. How much do you want to bet he's taught some of these students? I bet you anything he'd love to go to something like this." She sucked in a gasp. "What if I call the school and ask them? If Bart actually taught these kids, then they could do something to say thanks for everything he did."

"That's definitely an option." Olivia reached for the magazine. "And then when you guys are all made up, you could tell him he owes me." She winked at Izzie.

A small smile lit Izzie's face. If this worked, they'd both owe Olivia. Maybe they could find her someone special, too. For the first time in three days her heart felt a little bit lighter. She'd made this mess, and now she knew exactly how to fix it. She just hoped that Bart would accept her apology.

Chapter Twenty-Five

Bart glanced up as his secretary entered his office. She offered him a warm smile and deposited his messages on his desk. "I'm heading out for lunch. Can I get you anything before I go?"

He shook his head. "Enjoy your lunch." Bart reached for the first note and peered at it. "Jillian?"

She stopped in the doorway.

"I was invited to an art gallery event?"

"It appears so."

"Who dropped this off?"

Jillian frowned. "I'm not sure. It was on my desk when I got back from the break room."

Bart turned the ticket over in his hands. The event was tonight and he didn't really feel like going out. In fact, he'd made sure to stay away from social gatherings lately, Izzie's absence more painful than he'd like anyone to know.

The ticket didn't give any indication of what was being presented. He could probably just stay at home and no one would notice—except the person who'd purchased this ticket. He tossed the ticket on his desk and picked up the next note.

The first karaoke night at the casino was supposed to be next weekend. Another sharp pain accosted him. He'd hoped to have Izzie be the opening act to get the night started. But there was no way that would happen. She didn't want anything to do with him or the guitar he had bought her. That exact guitar that still sat in the corner of his office, collecting dust.

His gaze drifted toward the ticket again. He had been sulking far too long. Even Isaac had told him he needed to get out of his office and do something to get his mind off Izzie. If he didn't, where would that put him?

Bart picked up the ticket. Whoever had gotten this for him wanted him there for a reason. He might as well go if only to get his friend off his back.

Bart stepped from his limo and froze, the large banner over the entrance of the art gallery catching his attention. It big red letters the words *Johansson Art Gallery Proudly Presents the Graduating Class of Silverhawk Alternative High School.*

Chills raced down his spine and he glanced around at those entering the building. This wasn't a big show. The people in attendance weren't dressed to the nines, nor were they arriving in fancy vehicles. This show was strictly for the people who worked or attended the school.

Someone from the administration must have sent him an invitation. He smiled, an overwhelming feeling of nostalgia wrapping its warm arms around him. There were still people in this world who needed him and cared about him.

He strode toward the entrance, for once not being accosted by paparazzi or other photographers. Tonight was going to be far better than he had expected.

It would have been even better with Izzie by his side.

Bart pushed down the disappointing thought. Slipping through the double doors, he paused to soak it all in. There were several familiar faces near the entrance, welcoming the patrons. Various paintings and sculptures were showcased near the entrance but the way they were positioned, seemed to funnel the visitors one way through the gallery. He ducked behind a group of people as they continued moving farther into the gallery.

The artwork was amazing and as he moved along, progressing from one work to the next, he recognized several names of students he'd taught. He couldn't help but feel a great deal of pride. Some of the students had been struggling when he'd taught them and he had wondered how everything turned out when he'd taken on his current role.

A large group gathered in an open area surrounding a small platform. He stood in the back, waiting as several more people arrived. A young woman stood on the platform with a microphone in hand. She fidgeted with the cord, her eyes darting around the room.

Christina. That was her name. She'd been pregnant when he'd taught her at the age of fifteen. Back then, she was hardheaded and entitled. It appeared she had grown. The smile on her face was bright and while she looked nervous, there was a different kind of confidence about her.

A few more minutes passed and she brought the microphone to her lips. "Thank you all for coming tonight. I know a lot of us have worked really hard to get to where we are and we are so excited to share our art with you." Her eyes danced through the crowd. "Obviously, a lot of people come in and out of our lives and affect us at varying degrees. But even the ones who touch us for a small moment end up leaving us with lasting memories. I think it is safe to say that for most of us, there was one person who made the biggest difference in our lives. And I hope he is here tonight."

She glanced over to someone he didn't recognize on the side of the stage who shrugged and shook his head.

Her focus returned to the crowd. "Even if he wasn't able to attend, I wanted to say thank you and recognize him. Most of you might recognize him from the news or on TV. But I will always remember him as Mr. Bart."

Bart froze. His head whipped around, there was no disputing that she was talking about him. Nothing on the ticket had mentioned he'd be someone they highlighted.

Christine continued. "Mr. Bartholomew Brown was a substitute teacher long before he became the billionaire who everyone knows now. He was down to earth and he cared about his students. He was my favorite teacher and I was so sad when I found out he wasn't going to teach anymore. If you're here, would you mind coming on stage?"

It was as if his feet had a mind of their own. Slowly, he stepped toward the platform, the crowd in front of him dividing to let him through. Christine's eyes landed on him and she smiled brightly. Emotion shone in her eyes as she stepped to the side, giving him access to the platform.

The crowd erupted with cheers, clapping and whooping. Bart smiled and waved. Pride filled him so completely as he accepted the mic from Christine. "Wow. Hadn't expected this. Thank you all for this recognition. But it's not me that you should be cheering. These amazing kids are the ones who have worked hard to get to this point. They are the ones we are celebrating tonight." He gestured toward Christine and to the crowd before he clapped.

More cheers.

Bart took in a deep breath and let it out slowly. Tonight had been better than he could have predicted and for once he was grateful he'd opted to go out in public. Christine finished her speech and released the crowd to mingle then she turned to face Bart.

"I can't believe you came. She said she would get you the ticket and that you would come, but I wasn't sure." Christine's voice trembled with excitement. "We all thought you'd forgotten about us, but we never forgot you. Our whole school keeps tabs on the things you're doing." Her face flushed and she looked away. "I think all of us want to aspire to be more like you—all the charities and how you help the community."

"Wait. What were you saying? Someone brought me a ticket? Who were you talking to?"

Christine's brows creased and she frowned. "I don't remember. All I know is that the coordinator at the gallery asked me about you. I told her that you were one of our favorite teachers and she asked if we would like to invite you." Her smile returned, dimples filling her cheeks. "We're so glad you came."

Someone called her name and she turned around for a moment before facing him again. "I've got some people to visit with. But I'd really like it if you could take a picture with me in front of my sculpture."

"Sure."

She gave him an awkward hug then hurried away.

Still on the platform, Bart scanned the crowd. Whoever had invited him had known that he taught at that school which meant it was probably an administrator. That was the only likely person. It was nice of them to think of him and it had been just the thing to get him out of his own head about...

A familiar flash of red hair caught his attention and every part of his body froze up. The woman wasn't facing him and he couldn't be sure if it was Izzie who stood only a few feet away. He should leave, just slip out the building. He wasn't ready to speak to her yet. He needed the dust to settle just a little more.

Then she turned and suddenly he couldn't breathe. It was Izzie in all her beauty and grace. And on her neck was the jade heart. His tongue seemed to swell and his throat closed up as their eyes locked.

The whole room, the whole gallery, heck, even the whole world fell away at that moment. It was as if they had both been placed in a white empty space and all he could hear was the pounding of his heart and the way his breath left his lips.

Izzie tucked a curled strand of hair behind her ear and gave him a small smile. That had to be a good sign, right? She was here and she wasn't running from him, so he didn't have to either. He took a step down from the platform and walked toward her as she did the same.

Izzie's hands were clasped tightly in front of her and her gaze continued to bounce in other directions as if she couldn't bring herself to meet his eyes.

"Hey," she murmured softly.

"Hey."

"I'm glad you came."

Realization washed over him. "It was you. How did you know?"

She fidgeted in front of him, her voice so soft he nearly

didn't hear her words. "I didn't. I took a chance when I saw the announcement in the paper."

Bart hooked his finger under her chin, forcing her to lift her face so he could see it better. "Why?"

She pressed her lips together tightly and her chin trembled. "I'm so sorry." She sucked in sharply and shook her head. "I wanted to do something to show you that I love you and this was the best thing I could come up—"

His brows furrowed. This wasn't the reaction he'd expected from their first meeting after their break-up. Bart shook his head. "You don't have to apologize. You made it clear what you were comfortable with and I—I didn't listen." He offered her a wry smile. "Maybe I should have asked you before I did what I did." He glanced down at the necklace around her throat. "It's a beautiful piece. I'm glad it found its owner."

Izzie grasped the necklace with her fingertips and smiled softly. "Thank you. I think I'm beginning to understand you a little better." She made a face. "I still don't love the idea of you or anyone spending money on me—especially as much as you spent on this. But I'll try to be more open minded in the future."

He didn't have any words. Nothing he could say would express just how happy her words had made him.

Izzie's lashes fluttered and she laughed nervously. "Will you say something? Please?"

"What do you mean?" He couldn't help but let out a quiet chuckle.

She gave his shoulder a shove with her fingertips. "I don't know. Tell me that you forgive me or that we can get past this. Because living without you has been miserable." Izzie clamped her mouth shut and her face filled with a deep crimson color.

He reached for her, slipping his arms around her waist, he pulled her close. "I love you, Izzie. Nothing could change that." Bart pressed a gentle kiss to her forehead. "But there is one thing I should make clear. When I love someone, I want to be able to show that love in a way that makes sense. It won't always be gifts or spending money. But if there's a piece of jewelry that I think would look amazing on you or if there is a book I know you would love, I want to be able to get it for you—not because it's expensive but because I know you. I will always make sure my gifts are thoughtful and not just frivolously spending money. Do you suppose you could find that acceptable?"

Izzie's smile spread across her face. "If it means I can be with you, I'll try."

"Good."

Bart grasped the back of her head, tilting her face toward him as he pressed a firm kiss to her lips. The gallery had been a good start to an awful evening but having Izzie be the one to bring him here, showed him just how special their relationship had been. Their future together could only improve from this point forward.

Chapter Twenty-Six

"I can't believe I let you talk me into this. I'm not ready. I haven't sung in front of a crowd this big since... I don't remember when." Izzie hovered behind the stage at the casino, the guitar that Bart had given her in hand. Her legs trembled and her hands shook. She could barely catch her breath.

Bart held her face between both of his hands and stared directly into her eyes. "You can do this. I know you can. Don't forget, I've heard you practicing."

"But my song isn't even technically karaoke. It's a song I wrote."

"All the better to debut it here on my stage, don't you think?" His lips quirked up at the corners causing her stomach to knot further. "And after this, I'll take you out to Maple Gardens so you can do a private show for all of your fans out there."

It was times like this Izzie both loved and hated Bartholomew Brown. His calling—the substitute teaching career—was long gone, but he still utilized every last bit of his strategies to help those he loved and she fell into that department.

Her stomach lurched and she closed her eyes for a brief moment. "Okay. I can do this."

"Of course you can." His voice softened and she opened her eyes to find his loving gaze and reassuring grin. So much had changed over the last few weeks. It was still difficult to accept the gifts Bart loved to give, but she was getting better at it.

The parts she loved most were the quiet moments when they could be with each other without all of the chaos that came from being rich and famous. And that included this very moment.

Izzie let out a heavy sigh and shook her head. "Let's get this over with." She squared her shoulders and strode out on stage. The bright lights blinded her from seeing the throngs of people in the audience. This wasn't the typical karaoke night. Sure, Bart called it that, but there was a little more to it. People signed up and got to have the stage to themselves.

She perched on the stool that had been set up in the center of the stage and rested the guitar on her knee. Taking a deep, calming breath, she envisioned Bart's face and strummed the first chord.

The soft melody had a way of creeping through every shadowy place in her heart and healing her. The more she practiced the song, the happier she became. This was the moment of her life she'd always wanted but didn't dare hope she could have.

She'd been looking for a lost piece of jewelry and in the process found so much more. When the song ended, she reached up and grasped the jade necklace between her fingers.

The crowd erupted with applause and her eyes fluttered open. It was as if the world had disappeared for those small moments while she was encircled by the music she'd composed.

Izzie smiled and got to her feet. She waved at the audience and hurried off the stage, her heart beating faster than it should. Izzie collided with Bart, a hysterical laugh bubbling from her throat. "Did you see that? I can't believe I did that! It was such a rush."

He held her out in front of him by her upper arms, a wide grin on his face. "I knew you could do it. And tonight is only the first of many. I didn't tell you before, but I wanted to discuss whether you'd be interested in being the main attraction a few times a month."

Her eyes widened and she shook her head. "I can't—I'm not good en—"

Bart pointed his finger out toward the audience as the next performer brushed past them. "Do you hear that? They *love* you, Izzie. And one day you're going to see what they see. You're going to see what I see."

Emotion burned in the back of her throat. This man had a way of making her feel like she mattered more than anything in the world. Izzie threw her arms around his neck. "I love you so much."

He held her tightly and murmured. "I love you too."

True to Bart's promise, they headed straight for Maple Gardens after the show in his limousine. Izzie was still jittery. Adrenaline pumped through her veins at a speed she'd never experienced. And she had Bart to thank for all of it. The smile wouldn't leave her face.

Bart chuckled from his seat and reached for her hand. "You're going to have to relax at some point."

She squeezed his hand. "I don't think that is possible."

His laughter warmed her and she leaned into him. "I have something for you."

"You didn't have to get me anything. Don't you know that I hate getting gifts?"

Izzie snickered. "Be nice. It wasn't much. But I thought you'd like it." She reached for her purse and retrieved a small paperback book then held it out to him.

Bart's eyes widened and by the look on his face, it was clear he assumed it was the book he'd told her about.

She shook her head, placing her hand on the cover. "This one isn't from your uncle. It's from me."

His disappointment was short lived as a crooked smile touched his lips. Without a word he reached for the book and flipped it open to the first page. His eyes dipped to where she wrote the words, 'To the mockingbird in my life. You do nothing but make music for me.'

Izzie watched him read it, and immediately felt the flush fill her cheeks. "It's dumb, I know, but I didn't know what else—"

He reached forward and grasped the back of her head with his hand to pull her close. His lips crushed over hers, exploring the soft texture and trying to convey something he couldn't say. She melted into a puddle right there. Her whole body reacted to his touch in a way that she still couldn't get used to.

When he pulled back, she had to catch her breath. Bart touched his forehead to hers. "It's perfect, Izzie," he whispered. "Absolutely perfect and I wouldn't want it any other way. Thank you."

A lump formed in her throat and she nodded, unable to say anything else to him. Thankfully they pulled up to Maple Gardens. Otherwise she would have probably made a fool of herself by saying something stupid. Like how often she'd thought about a future with him—long term.

Several times she'd thought about mentioning the idea of marriage. But then she'd stopped herself. It was too soon, right? Besides, it had to be something he was comfortable discussing. What if he wasn't ready?

She shook off the insecurity. Yet again one more thing she had to work on when she was around him. They headed inside, Bart holding her hand tightly. His hand was unusually clammy but then again, it could be her own clamminess that had been transferred to him.

The performance here wouldn't be nearly as bad. She knew the folks here. And her mother would be in the audience. Still it was hard to calm her racing heart even as they moved their way through the facility.

Olivia waved at them from her place behind reception and hurried over. "Everyone is in the game room. They're all ready for you. How did your first show go?"

Izzie made a face, hating any time she had to brag about herself. But Bart jumped in before she could say a word. He kissed her temple and grinned. "What do you think? This is Izzie Davis we're talking about?"

Olivia gave her a pointed look as if to suggest that Izzie needed to lock this guy down and fast. She lifted a shoulder and mouthed the word, 'later' to her friend before Bart whisked her down a hallway that led them toward the game room. It was already set up with several rows of filled seats along with tables where even more residents sat. The second they entered, a cheer filled the room.

Izzie laughed and waved at her mother's friends. Her gaze swept through the room until they landed on Margaret. She sat with three other women Izzie couldn't place a name to. One of them was Isaac's mother, whom she'd only met once. And then there was Lawrence right at her side. Her mother held his hand tightly and leaned closer to him to say something.

It was nice to see her mother had made some friends. Izzie would have to be sure and introduce herself when her little performance was over.

Once again, she waved at the group of people but this time she introduced herself. "Hi! I'm Isobel Davis— Margaret's daughter." She glanced at Bart and grinned. "But those close to me call me Izzie. I'm going to play you some songs and later you can make requests."

More clapping.

This performance wasn't nearly as adrenaline inducing. The lights didn't block the audience from her view and they were all watching her with happy expressions. She loved being able to share her love with the people who had become her mother's new family.

When the small performance was over including the special requests, she headed over to her mother. "Looks like you've really gotten popular, Mom."

Her mother waved at her dismissively. "Oh, hush. These are just a few friends I've made. This is Millie, that's Alice, and that over there is Lily."

Izzie's focus landed on each of the older women and she smiled warmly. "Pleasure to meet you."

"The pleasure is ours." Millie winked at her. "We're happy to hear that you and Bartholomew have worked everything out."

Izzie stilled then she laughed. "What?"

"Oh, come now, dear. Do you honestly think you can stick a bunch of us old ladies in a place like this and we wouldn't pay attention to something like that? Watching you two get closer and hearing updates from your mother was sometimes the only entertainment we got." She glanced between her other friends. "But now that you two have worked out, we're going to need some new entertainment. How often did you say you could come play that guitar of yours?"

Izzie laughed again. "I'll see about putting something on the schedule more often."

Millie clapped her hands together. "That's simply wonderful."

Izzie turned to her mother. "Oh, I almost forgot. I wanted to give this back to you." She reached to unclasp her necklace. "It was so nice to borrow it for my first performance."

Margaret held up a hand. "Nonsense. You keep it."

Confusion flooded every part of Izzie, her hands slowly falling to her sides. "What? Why? It's yours."

She shook her head. "You know something? I've never really noticed just how well it matches your eyes. It couldn't be more perfectly suited for you." She reached out and took hold of Izzie's hand. "And it will look perfect on your wedding day."

Izzie's heart dropped to her stomach and she froze. Her mother made a gesture for Izzie to turn around. Chills swept through her whole body and she spun to find Bart on one knee right in front of her.

A gasp tore from her throat and her hands flew to cover her mouth.

Bart cocked his head slightly, "Isobel Davis, will you—"

Izzie flung herself at him, nearly causing him to lose his balance. She peppered his face with kisses in between each word she spoke. "Yes. Yes. Of course. I'll. Marry. You."

She vaguely heard Olivia's voice behind her murmur. "Finally."

Her sentiments exactly.

Epilogue

Bart kept his arm around Izzie's waist, unwilling to let her wander too far. She had made him the happiest man on the planet and he wanted to hold onto this feeling as long as possible. She chatted excitedly with Olivia as the two stared at the ring he'd picked out for her. It was a princess cut diamond—not too big, but still impressive. And the stones that lined the band were small jade stones.

He'd had it commissioned for her far earlier than he'd like to admit. It had just taken a little longer to get to him than he'd liked.

His grasp on her tightened and he nuzzled the hollow of her neck, earning himself a soft crooning sound that escaped her lips.

Olivia insisted that she was going to be the best maid of honor and once that conversation started, he tuned out. He was just content to be near her. That was all he wanted. His eyes swept through the room, landing on his uncle and Margaret.

A smile touched his lips. They had grown a lot closer than he'd expected. Margaret was good for Lawrence. One of the orderlies had mentioned that Lawrence had talked again. Again it was one word, but it was more than they had gotten since he'd first said Izzie's name.

A familiar figure moved across the room. Isaac headed straight for his mother, Millie. He leaned down and kissed his mother on the head then took a seat beside her. It wasn't often that Isaac was able to pay his mother a visit, but Bart had gotten him to do so more often and it had seemed to brighten Millie's spirits much more.

Olivia groaned. "Ugh. *He's* back."

Bart glanced toward Olivia to see where she might be looking and found her staring in the direction Isaac sat. His brows furrowed and he spoke at the same time as Izzie.

"Who? Isaac?"

She glanced between the two of them. "Yes. Do you guys know him?" Judgement laced her words.

"You *don't* know him?" Izzie laughed. "He's Bart's friend. And he's not that bad."

"Whatever you say. He wasn't so great the last time we interacted." She pulled out her phone. "Shoot. I have to get back to work." She gave Izzie a tight hug. "Congrats, girl."

"Thanks, Liv."

They both watched Olivia hurry across the room, passing Isaac and the group of women who visited near the exit. Isaac glanced in Olivia's direction, recognition written on his face as his eyes followed her out. His mother stopped her talking, her focus following her son's.

Bart chuckled. "Uh oh."

"What?" Izzie followed his gaze to where he was staring. "Did she say something to him?"

He shook his head. "No, it's nothing Olivia did. It's your mother's new friends."

She craned her neck to get a better view. "What about them? They seem really nice."

"Oh, they're nice all right. But they're a bunch of meddlers."

"What do you mean?"

Bart faced her. "Once when I was visiting Uncle Lawrence, I had an interesting conversation with Millie. She told me she's been interested in our budding relationship."

Izzie's cheeks pinked up and she glanced away with a soft giggle. "She said something similar to me."

"Well, then you might wonder what they're going to keep themselves busy with now that we're together."

"Yeah. They want me to perform more."

He shook his head and chuckled. "If you saw the way they watched Olivia as she passed, you wouldn't have even suggested that."

She stared at him blankly, clearly not understanding what he was getting at.

"They're a bunch of self-proclaimed matchmakers. They need a new mark. Who better than one of their own children? I'd bet my entire fortune that they push Isaac into a relationship with Olivia."

Izzie gave him a disbelieving smirk. "I think you're reading too much into what she must have said to you."

He shook his head once more. "Just you wait. Olivia and Isaac won't know what hit them." He wrapped his arms around the love of his life and whispered, "And I wish them the same happiness you've given me."

There are four books available in the Maple Gardens Matchmaker series. More information on Phillipa's website www.phillipaclark.com

About the Author

Phillipa lives just outside a beautiful town in country Victoria, Australia. She also lives in the many worlds of her imagination and stockpiles stories beside her laptop.

She writes from the heart about love, dreams, secrets, discovery, the sea, the world as she knows it... or wishes it could be. She loves happy endings, heart-pounding suspense, and characters who stay with you long after the final page.

With a passion for music, the ocean, animals, nature, reading, and writing, she is often found in the vegetable garden pondering a new story.

Free short book when you join Phillipa's monthly newsletter (book chat, pets, gardens, puzzles, first-looks and competitions).

www.phillipaclark.com

Also by Phillipa Nefri Clark

Detective Liz Moorland

Lest We Forgive

Lest Bridges Burn

Lest Tides Turn

Connected to this series through several characters is

Last Known Contact

Rivers End Romantic Women's Fiction

The Stationmaster's Cottage

Jasmine Sea

The Secrets of Palmerston House

The Christmas Key

Taming the Wind

Temple River Romantic Women's Fiction

The Cottage at Whisper Lake

The Bookstore at Rivers End

The House at Angel's Beach

Charlotte Dean Mysteries

Christmas Crime in Kingfisher Falls

Book Club Murder in Kingfisher Falls

Cold Case Murder in Kingfisher Falls

Plan to Murder in Kingfisher Falls

Festive Felony in Kingfisher Falls

Daphne Jones Mysteries

Daph on the Beach

Time of Daph

Till Daph Do Us Part

The Shadow of Daph

Tales of Life and Daph

Bindarra Creek Rural Fiction

A Perfect Danger

Tangled by Tinsel

Maple Gardens Matchmakers

The Heart Match

The Christmas Match

The Menu Match

The Cookie Match

Doctor Grok's Peculiar Shop Short Story Collection

Simple Words for Troubled Times

(Short non-fiction happiness and comfort book)

———